HOLIDAY HOPE

A HOLIDAY ROMANCE NOVEL
BOOK 6

AMANDA SIEGRIST

MERRY CHRISTMAS.

MAY YOUR DAYS AND NIGHTS BE FILLED WITH HOLIDAY CHEER!

1

————

"Merry Christmas. Happy Holidays. What can I do for you this joyous day?"

Giggles erupted on the other end of the line. "Who is this and what did you do with my sister?"

Hope rolled her eyes at her sister Chasity and the snort she heard through the phone.

"What are you laughing at?"

"I have never heard you sound so...merry."

Hope slid her finger through the coil of the phone cord and started to twist it around her finger. "Well, it's two weeks before Christmas, so why not be merry?" Not to mention she worked at St. Paul's Cathedral and she wanted to send the right message when people called. She could be joyful and cheerful if she put her mind to it. It crushed her that her sister thought she couldn't be pleasant, especially answering the phone.

Although, in Chasity's defense, Hope had been a bear the last few months. Sometimes Chasity had to tiptoe around her and her emotions. Not something she wanted to think about.

"What's up?" Hope asked when Chasity didn't respond to her last comment.

"Stu and I were talking this morning about Christmas. We were thinking we'd spend Christmas Eve with Grandpa in the afternoon and then have something at our house on Christmas Day. Does that sound good to you? We were going to invite Dad and Stu's parents."

Hope couldn't control her groan.

"I know, I know. Stu's dad is trying to be nicer."

Hope rolled her eyes but didn't respond. That man didn't know the meaning of nice. She had worked for him long enough to know exactly the kind of asshole he was. Sure, he was the mayor of the town—most people didn't see the meanness behind the facade he portrayed—but she knew the truth. The only reason he was cozying up to Stu—his own son—was to get him heavily on his side as he ran for governor. Elections were coming up next year for the governor position. He started his promoting last year, trying to weasel his way into the people's good graces. She didn't trust the guy.

"Hope?"

She didn't want to put a damper on Chasity's plans, and despite the turmoil going on inside her, she was trying to make this a good holiday. Not one with her wallowing in ridiculous pity.

"Yeah, sounds awesome. I'll be there."

"We can—"

"No, it'll be great. I promise. No changing plans. I'll be on my best behavior."

Maybe. She shouldn't promise that. She had a wild streak she couldn't control sometimes. She'd been called a drama queen more times than she could count on one hand. By teachers, by her mother, by her sister, and countless others she didn't even want to name. Whatever. She was who she was and people would have to deal with it. But she could at least attempt to be pleasant for Chasity's sake.

Chasity chuckled. "Let's try to grab lunch later this week. I miss you."

She returned the sentiment, promised her sister they'd catch up later, and hung up. It was ridiculous how much she missed Chasity as well. They lived in a small town. It was hard not to run into the same person at least once a week. Yet she hadn't seen her sister in two weeks. Not since the beginning of the month when they bought trees together. One for Stu's house—where Chasity now lived with him— and one for her apartment. She had taken over Chasity's lease when she moved out. The place she lived last year had become too expensive when she quit her job working for the asshole mayor. It had been a blessing her sister let her live with her. Three months after dating Stu, she moved out and let Hope take over the lease.

Her place hadn't been as expensive. Within those few months, she had found a new job at the church. Eileen— longtime secretary for Father Benson—had finally retired. It had been perfect timing for her. Running an office was what Hope did best. She liked the organization, the day-to-day details of keeping everything on track. It proved to her she could keep things together when her private life was nothing but utter chaos.

"Knock, knock."

Hope glanced at her doorway where Father Benson stood with a bright smile on his face. She swore the man never frowned. It helped the happiness suffocating inside her seep out in little pockets. She loved his positive, joyful attitude.

"Oh, I like the headband this morning."

She touched the reindeer headband she put on this morning and grinned. Her attempt at faking happiness started today. And what better way to do that than prove she could be as merry as the rest of them. She decided for the next two weeks before Christmas, she'd show her holiday spirit with finesse. She had a ton of crap at home. Kind of like a hoarder. The amount of Christmas paraphernalia she had wasn't something a normal person owned. She was glad Father Benson approved. It would've dampened her spirits if he told her not to wear it.

"Thanks. I contacted Lynn already and she will have ten dozen cookies ready for the Sunday brunch. They will be delivered bright and early that morning."

"Oh, I do love her goodies. Thank you, Hope, dear. The contractor to fix the Nativity will be here in a little bit. Can you make sure he has everything he needs? I want that fixed as soon as possible. Just terrible what happened."

For a brief moment, Father Benson's brows puckered, yet a short smile remained. She wouldn't exactly describe it as *just terrible* what happened. She'd say it was downright the shittiest thing that could happen two weeks before Christmas. Of course, she'd never swear in front of a priest—or inside a church. It was hard at times to curb her tongue, but she prevailed. Sinning inside a church was the last thing she wanted to do.

Last night, some drunken idiot had crashed into the Nativity sitting in front of the church, destroying the beautiful scenery. It wasn't a small Nativity either. It crushed the figures standing around the manger where Christ lay, who, in some small miracle, had been spared any damage. But the three wise men and a lamb needed to be replaced along with the frame for the Nativity. Unfortunately, it had been a hit-and-run. Chief Duncan was looking into the crime himself. She had already spoken to him this morning as well about the incident. She even offered to call the contractor to fix the Nativity, but he said he knew someone and would take care of it. It had bothered her she couldn't do it herself, but Father Benson had been standing there and agreed and she hadn't wanted to argue with a priest.

"I'm on it, Father. Don't you worry about a thing."

His smile emerged even brighter. "I never do when I know you're in charge. I'll see you after mass."

She nodded and waved good-bye, thankful she didn't have to go to mass. She was good about going to Sunday mass—some weekends, anyhow—but she couldn't do daily mass. It was a good thing she was needed at her desk.

Time to make sure the Nativity was put back to rights as soon as possible. Hope picked up the phone and dialed Betty's Craft Corner without looking up the number. She wouldn't say she had a wonderful memory, but she knew pretty much every number for each business in town. One of the perks she acquired working for the mayor's office. He might've worked her to the bone, but it also helped her learn the ins and outs of how the town was run. She missed it some days. The day-to-day intricacies of how the town ran, not the mayor himself. He could go sit on a stick and rotate for all she cared.

"Betty's Craft Corner. Merry Christmas. How may I help you on this beautiful day?"

Ha! See, she wasn't the only one merrily answering the phone.

"Hey, Betty, it's Hope. I need three wise men and a lamb."

Sweet, musical laughter floated to her ear. She knew Betty would have heard what happened at the church—as most of the town probably already knew—so explaining why she needed what she did wouldn't be necessary. It did sound comical and like the start of a good joke. Except, what was the punch line?

"I figured you'd be calling me sooner or later. I put in a rush order. It should be here in two days, at the latest. Fingers crossed for tomorrow."

"You are a lifesaver. Thank you. Send me the invoice and I'll pay it straight away."

"Heavens, no. This is on me. You tell Father Benson not to worry about a thing."

Aww, the joys of living in a small town. People could be so generous.

"I'm sure he sends his thanks. It's very kind of you. Thank you."

She hung up with Betty, feeling even better about the situation. Two days wasn't very long to wait for the new pieces to the Nativity. While Betty sold a wide range of crafts galore, she also sold Christmas decorations of all varieties. When people wanted to decorate their home, Betty's was the place to go. Well, the large, sometimes gaudy outdoor decorations, anyway. Lights and other little Christmas trinkets could also be purchased at Bernie's Hardware Store. But for what she needed, Betty was her gal.

Needed a tree? Jeff's Tree Lot had the best around these parts. Baked Goods? Lynn's Sweet Treat Delights could beat out any place with flying colors. They might live in a small town—full of annoying gossip—but it was a pretty damn awesome town. She wouldn't want to live anywhere else, despite how she felt lately, wanting to escape.

Another knock on her doorframe had her popping her head up. If she hadn't been sitting down in her chair, she would've fainted and fallen at the sight in front of her.

Mase Brandt.

Sexiest man to ever walk into her life—and out of it.

"Hey, Hope."

Shit on a stick.

Just her luck.

"I'm here to build a Nativity set."

Of course he was. Because he was the best damn carpenter around these parts. She should've known when Chief Duncan said he'd take care of it that he'd call Mase.

The one thing that had made her life hell the last few months stood right in front of her.

She had fallen in love and had her heart broken all in one fell swoop.

MASE TRIED to breathe normally and act like seeing her again wasn't a big deal

Oh, but it was.

Huge deal.

This woman had stolen his heart with one wicked smile and he had yet to get it back from her—even with the fallout they had a few short months ago. He wasn't sure where it all went wrong.

Of course, he wasn't sure it even started out right.

He waited patiently for her to say something. He might've started the conversation—despite it being professional in nature—but he'd wait for her to continue it. It didn't matter how long it would take either. The way he still felt, he'd wait for an eternity and beyond for this woman. For her heart. For her laughter. For her to accept him and let him in.

"We need a new frame. Like yesterday."

He nodded. The destruction sitting outside wasn't pretty.

Since it was such a large piece, it would be easier to build it right on-site rather than building it back in his workshop and hauling it here.

It was cold as shit outside.

"I want to run down some particulars with you—or Father Benson. Make sure exactly what you want."

Her eyes dilated and her lips thinned.

Maybe she took his last words to mean more than just the new Nativity set. Like, what did she want? Because the last time he asked her that, she couldn't give him a clear answer. Then she disappeared from his life and he let her. It had been one of the hardest things he had ever done letting her walk away without a fight.

"Would you like to speak to Father Benson about it instead of me?"

He barely managed to remain still and not jerk back as if she had slapped him hard across the face. *That* was what she took out of what he said. That he didn't even want to deal with her? Wow. Just. Wow.

That wasn't what he had meant to insinuate at all. He simply threw it out there for her sake, in case she didn't want to deal with him. Obviously, he'd have to choose his words carefully from now on.

"No."

Since he wasn't sure what the right words might be, saying as little as possible seemed like the best option. Short and simple.

Her eyes narrowed.

And apparently, he couldn't get anything right when it came to her.

An audible sigh escaped before she spoke. "The same type of frame will be fine. The manger was busted as well, so we'll need a new one of those, too. How soon can you have it done?"

If he could've said right this second, he would've, to put a smile on her face.

"A few days. I'll do my best to get it done as soon as I can."

Her frown increased.

Well, there wasn't much he could do to turn that frown upside down. He wasn't a miracle worker. Cam—his business partner and best friend—was busy on a few other projects. Two of those had been his until Chief Duncan called asking for a favor. It was hard to turn Chief Duncan down when he got him out of a sticky situation this past summer. The same situation that had involved Hope and her nasty ex, who he thankfully hadn't seen since.

Not to mention, he didn't feel comfortable turning down a priest asking for help either.

"Send me the invoice ASAP and I'll take care of it."

"It's on the house."

Her beautiful hazel eyes narrowed once again.

"Why?"

"Why not? It's almost Christmas."

"We'll pay the bill, thank you."

"It's not technically for you. It's for the church. And I don't mind donating my time for the church."

A flash of pain flickered in her gaze. As if she took his words wrong again. That he did mind donating his time for her. Oh, how wrong she was.

"I'm sure Father Benson will be grateful for your kindness."

They stared at each other for a long moment. He ached to ask her out—again—for the billionth time. Yet, rejection got old after a while. It hurt, too.

"I guess I'll get to it."

She nodded.

He left her office, hating to walk away without asking what had gone wrong with them. Yet, he kept walking because, in the end, he knew she wouldn't tell him a damn thing.

The coldness wrapped around him and slapped him in the face as soon as he walked back outside. Single digits and he was going to be working outside in it the next few days. Oh, how merry it would be.

Instead of heading for his truck, he took long, quick strides to the Nativity scene where Chief Duncan stood.

"Chief."

"Hey, Mase. Thanks for coming so quickly. We appreciate it."

He shoved his gloved hands inside his coat pockets and nodded. "Not a problem. I can't believe some jackass even ran into this and then left."

"Probably drunk. Or not paying attention. Either way, they didn't want to get in trouble."

"Think you'll find who did it?"

Chief Duncan shrugged. "I'll try my best, but so far, not having much luck. There are a few scrapes of paint on some of the wood, suggesting it was a red vehicle. The snow is too churned up to decipher a specific tire tread. There are no security cameras in front of the church here. I'll check out the few in the area and see if they caught anything. Maybe erratic driving, or a busted-up vehicle. It'll be hard to pin down, but I'll do my best to find the culprit. How long do you think it'll take you to rebuild?"

Mase looked at the broken pieces and how large the piece used to be. At least twenty feet long and five feet deep. He didn't want to use plain wood either. He'd need it to be protected for the outdoor elements. Normally, he'd stain and do all the intricate work himself, but since they wanted it so fast, he'd use prefinished wood.

"A few days. It'll be just me. Cam is working on quite a few other projects."

Chief Duncan nodded as if he understood he was taken away from some of those other projects.

"Let me know if you need any help."

"Thanks. Do you need any of this before I haul it away? I don't know. Evidence wise."

"I got what I needed. But I'll help you load it into your truck if you like."

"I'd appreciate it."

He retrieved a few hammers and other tools from his truck before dismantling the old frame for the nativity set. They worked in silence, but with an easy rhythm where they had it broken into pieces where it'd fit comfortably in the back of his truck in no time.

His fingers tingled from the cold as he slammed the tailgate shut.

"I'll be back as soon as I drop this off and grab the supplies I need."

"I'll check in on you. Help where I can." Chief Duncan grinned. "I'll bring some of Theresa's famous coffee."

Mase chuckled. Before the fight that had landed him in jail for a night, he had tasted a cup of her java. Not the best he'd ever had, but he had been told by Hope it was sort of a thing in this small town. Theresa's terrible coffee.

"I can't wait."

Chief Duncan twisted as if about to walk away, then his brows pleated before speaking. "You talk to Hope yet?"

"Before I came out here."

Mase wasn't sure where the chief was going with this

conversation, so he decided to let him lead it. The last thing he wanted to do was put his foot in his mouth with the man who could lock him up again.

He had met Hope at the hardware store. He'd been buying some new tools he had needed, she had been buying some wallpaper for her bathroom. One smile had been all it took for him to fall in love. He'd never been one of those guys who believed in love at first sight. But boy, with one look from her, it was as if he had been knocked on his ass, jolted with a bout of love. He couldn't explain it. He didn't even want to try and figure it out. It was the first time in his life he went with the flow. Let his heart lead him for once.

Conversation flowed easily and it had broken his heart to know she was married. Or at least, that's what she told him at first. While he wouldn't consider himself a stalker, he had ventured to Mulberry more times than he could count in the few days leading up to the fight at the diner, hoping for a glimpse of her. Another chance to talk to her—married or not. He also never thought of himself as a home-wrecker, but there was something about Hope that made him unable to stay away. His chance finally came when he saw her in the diner and took a seat next to her, playing it off as if both of them being there had been by chance. And it partly had been. He hadn't known she'd be there; it had been pure luck. To his surprise, she confessed to lying about being married—although never gave him a reason why—and before he could inquire more, her ex showed up. One thing led to another and he was suddenly involved in a fistfight with the guy. A call to his brother Jaxson in New York had Jaxson calling Chief Duncan, who he happened to know, and the charges were dropped. Although the judge had said to stay out of Mulberry. That lasted about a month before the same judge had called him looking for a new deck.

The last time he had seen Hope was when she came to Mason to thank him for sticking up for her when her ex, Tyrone, had caused problems. Despite asking her to go out with him again—something he had tried in the diner and in the hardware store—she had declined and left. It had torn his heart out. He honestly wasn't sure how to proceed with her.

They had talked a long time that day. About life and everything in between. It was when he asked 'what do you want' concerning where her life was going since she quit her job that she clammed up on him and left shortly after. He scared her somehow and he wished ever since then he could take his words back. Perhaps she would've said yes to his desperate attempt to keep her in his life when he asked her to dinner. A simple dinner. That's all he wanted. And she refused as if he had asked to marry her instead.

Maybe the chief would know how to proceed with Hope.

But sort of an awkward question to ask someone he barely knew.

"Her ex leaving her alone?"

A good place to start, he figured.

"I haven't seen him around town, so I'd say yes. Hope is a tough one. She can handle herself."

"I don't trust the guy."

"Neither do I. I've been keeping an eye out for him. We look out for each other in this town." Chief Duncan smiled. "I like you, Mase. I'll see you later."

Hmm. Odd. But whatever, he'd take it. It was better to be on the chief's good side.

As long as Tyrone wasn't bothering Hope, that's all that mattered.

Not even his broken heart mattered. As long as she was happy, it made him happy.

2

_____

SHE TWISTED her lips as she stared at the blue concoction in front of her.

"What is this beauty before me?"

Stu, her sister's fiancé, grinned as he leaned against the counter behind him. "A Coconut Snowball Martini. You looked like you needed something to cheer you up?"

Taking a sip, she could feel a bout of happiness settle in her stomach. At least, from the sweet drink.

"This is delicious. Just what the doctor would've ordered."

Stu laughed. "Care to share your woes?"

With her future brother-in-law? Not really. Talk about awkward. Although, she was pretty tight with him. He was a cool guy. He loved her sister like the world revolved and ended with only her. Her parents' marriage wasn't anything to brag about. The only mark against Stu was *his* parents—his father specifically. Considering Stu didn't get along with him either, she couldn't hold it against him.

"It's nothing. I'm having a pity party with myself."

She had no one to blame about anything but herself.

The things with Mase—or lack thereof—were her fault. That broken heart that she couldn't seem to fix. Her fault.

Everything was her fault.

"I heard Mase is in town building the Nativity set."

She cocked a brow and took another sip.

"He seems like a nice guy."

Ugh. That was an understatement. He was the sweetest, kindest guy she had ever met.

But she had terrible judgment in men. One after another, loser, loser, loser. That's all she ever dated. Look at her last one—Tyrone. Obsessive, controlling jerk.

She didn't trust her judgment. Her gut when she first met Mase in the hardware store had told her he was a decent guy. Of course, her gut had told her that a million times before. She couldn't trust the dumb thing. Before she could stop herself, she was blurting she was married just to keep him at a distance. No need to lead a guy on when she had sworn men off.

She ruined her chances with him before they even began. Now she feared she let the best thing to walk into her life walk right back out.

"That's right." Stu snapped his fingers. "You're as stubborn as your sister."

Hope laughed. "When is my darling sister getting here? I swore she told me eight o'clock, and she's still missing in action."

After promising they'd get together for lunch later in the week, she had decided she needed to see Chasity sooner and asked to meet up for drinks tonight. Chasity was never late. She was the punctual one. The organized one. The Bronson girl who had her shit together.

Hope was the disorganized, dysfunctional, screwing everything up one. Drama queen galore.

Stu shrugged. "She told me she had to run errands today, which I took as code for buying presents, and I haven't spoken to her since she ran out the door this morning."

"I hope she got me something good this year."

A familiar hand clapped her on the back as Stu and Chasity's laughter circled the air. "Like a happy wand. I wave it, and you'll magically smile for me."

Hope rolled her eyes at Chasity as she finally sat down next to her.

Okay. So she might've been a bit moody the past month or so. Whatever. She couldn't help it. Her emotions had been all over the place the past year. It all started last Christmas when she quit her job because she couldn't stand working for the mayor and his dictatorial ways. And especially after the way he treated her sister. It's as if her life had been flowing semi-smoothly and then took a drastic turn and nothing but turbulent waters ahead of her.

"Where have you been?"

"Like Stu said." Chasity narrowed her eyes in a playful way. "No searching the house for stuff either, mister."

Stu held up his hands in surrender. "Scout's honor."

"You were never a scout," Chasity said with a chuckle as he walked away to help someone at the other end of the bar.

Hope nearly rolled her eyes again when her sister pinned that *look* at her. Sisterly concern, sympathy...maybe a bit of pity thrown in there. So frustrating. That's not what she wanted from her sister at all. Hell, Hope had no idea what she wanted from anyone, even herself. She felt so lost and had for the longest time.

"Talk to me." Chasity licked her lips. "While I steal a sip of whatever you have."

Hope chuckled and pushed the Snowball concoction

closer to her sister, who took a sip—more like a gulp—of the yummy drink.

"Mase is in town building a new frame for the Nativity." She grabbed the napkin near her and started to tear the corner off. "He's nearly done with the frame. He's so good at what he does."

"I saw him working outside. He was moving fast. Probably due to the cold." Chasity laughed.

Of course, it sounded forced. Chasity was trying to cheer her up, even though she didn't know why she had to cheer her up.

"What's wrong with me?"

"That is a very broad question." Chasity made a funny face, trying to elicit another laugh out of her. Her smile fell. "Look, I know you tend to gravitate towards the..." Chasity shook her head back and forth, looking for the right word. "Douchebags."

Hope snorted, her eyes widening at her sister's audacity. "You did not just say that."

"Truth hurts, sis. Don't deny it. Ugh. Dale cheated on you. Roger stole from you. Matt couldn't keep a job. Tony drank too much. And Tyrone," Chasity shook her head, "he could've gotten physical if you hadn't broken it off when you did."

That was no exaggeration on her part. The last fight she and Tyrone had, he had grabbed her by the arm. If not for her friend Charlie teaching her a few defense moves, Tyrone might've done more damage than simply grabbing her arm so roughly. He had snatched her arm so hard, it left a bruise. When she twisted out of his grasp, she left her own nice bruise on his face. Fair was fair. That had been the end of them. She had dumped his ass and moved on, even if he had a problem understanding that in the beginning.

She had never told Chasity about the incident. It had been better to keep it to herself than let her sister worry over something that would never happen again. Because she wouldn't let it.

Thank goodness for Charlie and his forethought, saying every woman needed to know how to defend themselves. Maybe she didn't have completely bad taste in men. She dated Charlie for about a month. Great guy. Good in bed. Good job as a local firefighter. Except, no real chemistry. Neither one had that undying spark of something amazing between them, so they amicably broke up and remained friends. Out of all the losers she dated, he was the only good breakup.

"Mase seems like a good guy."

She couldn't dispute that either.

"You met him so close to breaking it off with Tyrone. You were going through a lot with that shithole."

Hope giggled. Her sister rarely used silly swear words. Only she did. Hope looked at her.

"What are you saying?"

"I'm saying it couldn't hurt to give the guy a chance. Chief Duncan likes him. That seems like a big stamp of approval in my book."

Hope dragged her drink back to her side, side-eyeing her sister as if saying 'try and take it back.' "I ruined my chances with him. I lied when I first met him, saying I was married. He probably assumed it was Tyrone when the asshole came jumping in the picture."

"Oldest trick in the book—feign marriage when you don't want a guy hitting on you. Again, you were coming out of a bad relationship. He shouldn't hold that against you."

Hope took a large sip, nearly depleting the drink. Although, her sister had taken a good chunk out of it as well. "He didn't. At least, I don't think he did. I never explained why I said I was married. I'm hopeless. I don't do relationships well."

Chasity smiled at her, then adjusted her reindeer antlers on her head. "You're not hopeless. You're Hope. Grab them by the balls, take no shit, eat them for breakfast, Hope."

Another snort came out as she shook her head at her sister and her bold, crazy words.

"So he's asked you out a few times and he might not again for fear of rejection. Maybe he's moved on."

Hope frowned. "Wait, where did the encouraging speech go? Go back to that one. This one sucks."

More sweet laughter filled the air. "I just told you who you are. So what he won't ask you out again. Ask him out. Because the Hope I know and love doesn't sit around on her ass waiting for shit to happen. She makes it happen."

Chasity snatched her drink, draining the last of its contents. "Remember last year when you up and quit your job in support of me. Not everyone does that. Only strong people do that. Only people who know what they want and what they believe in do that."

Well, she wasn't so sure about that. She didn't know what she wanted—in any aspect of her life.

"And if he says no and breaks my heart further?"

"Then he doesn't deserve you."

This was what she needed. Her sister and her wisdom. Her undying support and words of encouragement. For Chasity just to listen to her and know she cared.

"Order up."

She looked at Stu and the two new drinks sitting in front of them. Still a martini glass, but this time with a light golden-brown color. Oh, a surprise drink. She had enjoyed the Snowball martini.

Chasity smiled, winked, and leaned across the bar for a kiss. Hope lifted her drink and said thanks.

"What is this one?"

"Nothing fancy this time. A chocolate martini, but I know you two love your chocolate."

Ugh. Her sister had the best guy in the world. Knew Chasity inside and out. Hell, he even knew her likes and dislikes.

That's what she wanted.

That's what she craved.

The question was...

Was Mase that guy for her?

———

ANOTHER SHIVER RIPPLED THROUGH HIM, yet he ignored it. He had no choice. This frame for the Nativity set had to be finished, then he had to work on the manger for baby Jesus. Although, technically that one he could work on in his shop where it was warm and toasty, and then deliver it.

He liked being close to Hope, despite not actually seeing her. Yesterday, besides talking to her briefly in her office, he hadn't seen her again. Today, no such luck either. It was nearing lunchtime and he hadn't seen a wink of her. As much as he wanted to catch a glimpse of her, he had no reason to go knock on her door for anything.

The frame was almost done, so he could go tell her that. One quick peek. Even if she did frown at him.

Mase couldn't get a good read on her. It bugged him. Hot and cold, since the moment he met her. Sending mixed signals so much that his stomach was tied in knots wondering and worrying if he had a chance.

Considering he hadn't seen her in a few months, he was going with no chance whatsoever.

He set his hammer down when his phone went off. Groaning at the thought of taking off his gloves to answer it, he did it anyway.

"What's up, Cam?"

"You done yet?"

Although his friend asked with a teasing tone, he knew he was serious.

"Getting there. I should be done tomorrow with everything."

He didn't add it would be closer to mid-afternoon or evening when he'd be done, but whatever. Cam knew. Hell, getting this all done within two days was amazing. Not everyone would be able to do it. But he wasn't just anyone. He was someone who loved working with wood. Creating masterpieces and doing intricate stuff. Some said—his mother mostly—he had magic in his hands. He'd take the compliment. He took pride in his work. When he had a project, no matter the kind, even something simple like changing the trim around the baseboard of a room, he put his whole mind and energy into it. Nothing but the best was good enough for him.

"Good. I need help, man. Mr. Stenson is being a real hard-ass about this kitchen remodeling. He has a party this weekend and expects it to be done tomorrow. That shit ain't happening, even if you were here to help me right now."

Mase rolled his eyes. Mr. Stenson had been a pain in their ass since the moment he called last week wanting his kitchen done. Their schedule was slammed, yet he paid extra to get squeezed in before the holidays. They were doing the best they could, considering the circumstances.

"Look, when I'm done here, I'll head to Diana's Diner

and put in those new shelving units they wanted in the back. You concentrate on Mr. Stenson, and I got the rest."

"That's a lot of work for you. It can't be easy working in the cold."

Shit. That was an understatement.

"We can't afford to get a bad review from him, even though he's creating most of the problems, expecting us to be fast and do quality work at the same time. I got this. Don't worry about it. I'm almost done with the frame. Then it's just the manger. Why don't you call Tim for some help? He could use the extra money around the holidays."

Cam groaned.

Yeah, Mase understood. Tim wasn't the best when it came to using a hammer. The last time they put one in his hand, he smashed his thumb. But he was good at being a gopher, getting supplies and tools, and following directions. It would help out Cam, and he knew it.

"Yeah, you're right. Stay warm, dude. Call me later."

Mase hung up with Cam, grateful to put his gloves back on. He picked up his hammer and almost dropped it when Hope appeared out of nowhere.

"Hey."

He couldn't stop the beaming smile on his face. "Hi."

Keep it cool. Don't say anything stupid.

"Here. I thought this might warm you up some. You've been out here all morning."

She held out a disposable cup with a lid. He took it, a bit of giddiness filling him up. She approached him first when he'd been dying to do it all morning.

What took her so long?

You've been out here all morning.

Did that mean she had been watching him out of one of the windows? He could only hope.

"Thanks." He took a sip. A jolt of warmth spread throughout his body. His brow arched. "This is more than just hot chocolate."

A silly smile spread across her lips. "Maybe I added a dash of Baileys."

He chuckled, then took another sip. "And a candy cane." Because he tasted a peppermint flavor as well.

"More like a shot of peppermint schnapps."

More laughter fell out.

"You brought a bunch of liquor to church."

"Well, it's not like Father Benson keeps it in stock. It's colder than a witch's clit out here. I thought it might warm you up."

"You mean tit?" He laughed.

This time a sly smile twisted her lips. "That's what I said. Colder than a witch's tit."

But by the teasing glint in her eyes, she had meant what she said the first time.

Hope was flirting with him. Was he dreaming? Did he accidentally knock himself in the head with his hammer?

What was going on? She was being nice and bringing him a delicious drink. One that he had to admit was warming him up inside. Making him feel all tingly, and not just in his stomach, but a bit below the belt as well.

She bit her bottom lip, her smile still on display. Then she glanced at the frame. "You're making good headway. I'm surprised."

Well, like she said, it was cold as shit outside. The faster he got it completed, the better it was for him.

Her cheeks bloomed a rosy red, and he didn't think it was from the brutal cold when she said, "I didn't mean that in a bad way. I know you're good at what you do. I guess I meant because it's only you out here. I thought it might take longer."

"It's a pretty simple frame, so it's not too involved."

It was about twenty feet long and five feet deep. One long wall with two short sides and a slatted roof. Just enough to make it look sort of like a barn. Enough to shelter the figurines that went along with the Nativity scene.

"So, you don't need any help? Father Benson is so grateful for your quickness in getting it back up."

He wasn't sure what to make of her bringing up Father Benson. Was she out here asking to help because Father Benson told her to do so? Or because she wanted to on her own?

"I'm good. The hot chocolate was nice of you. I appreciate it."

She nodded, a beautiful smile still gracing her face, yet the flirtiness behind it was gone. Maybe he misinterpreted her earlier behavior. Maybe he was making more out of something that was nothing but kindness. His poor, pitiful heart hoping for more when it wasn't really there.

He took another sip, this time more of a gulp. The hot liquid slid down his throat soothingly, filling up his cold veins. Super thoughtful idea by her. The splash of Baileys had a nice touch to it as well.

"So, your ex isn't bothering you, right?"

Her smile disappeared in a flash.

Great.

He told himself not to say something stupid and he went ahead and did it anyway.

"He's not."

He bobbed his head up and down, feeling stupider as the moment dragged on. Although, it crossed his mind more times than he cared to admit whether her ex was keeping his distance. He might not have a chance with Hope, but that didn't mean he didn't want her to be happy—and safe. That guy had been nothing but bad news.

"Good."

She raked her teeth over her bottom lip.

"I have terrible taste in men." She rolled her eyes. "I don't know why I said that."

He grinned, liking that she was so honest. Maybe not all the time, but she had moments where the truth blurted out. In his few short dealings with her, he'd come to find the most random things popped out of her mouth. It was adorable rather than annoying in his eyes.

There was something about her. He still couldn't explain it, even to himself, what that something was. All he knew was he loved this woman. Crazy and indescribable, for sure. Didn't matter one bit, though. He was going to accept the emotion for what it was and go with it.

"I'm not one of the bad ones."

One corner of her lip tilted upward. "Are you sure?"

"Pretty positive."

"That didn't sound one hundred percent sure."

He cracked his own sultry grin that he knew she could display so well. "I'm one hundred percent positive I'm a good guy. All you have to do is give me a chance."

Shit. Here he was going again. Putting his heart on the line for her to stomp all over it once again.

But he couldn't help it. She was like a drug he needed to breathe. One look and he was a goner. Her smile filled up the empty part of his heart that had been vacant for the longest time. He could honestly say it had never been filled by anyone yet. No woman had ever come close to it, and he had dated quite a few that almost had a chance.

She looked down at the white ground and shook her head.

Down for the count—again.

Her eyes found his.

"What are you doing later tonight?"

Working, working, working.

Shit.

She wasn't denying him. And he was so overloaded with work, he couldn't possibly put any of it aside.

"Not much."

But he couldn't let this slide. He couldn't let this opportunity slip through his fingers.

She tilted her head to the side and stared at him for the longest time. Maybe he should've said something else. Like 'I'm totally free.' Something that didn't seem so broad and like he didn't care either way if he hung out with her.

"I'm sorry. You'll be tired from working all day. We can get together another day."

"Tonight's good for me."

No way in hell he was letting her get out of it now.

He tossed his head toward the frame. "I have to make the manger. I was going to do it in my shop. You want to help?"

"You just said you didn't have much to do tonight."

His heart started to pound. Shit. He was muddling this up left and right.

"Doing this kind of stuff isn't like work to me. I enjoy building things. It calms me down."

"You puzzle me, Mase."

He chuckled. "Ditto, Hope."

Her lips widened into a beautiful smile. "I'd love to help. If you don't mind."

"Not at all."

This day went from cold to hot in the span of a few

minutes. If he was really lucky, it'd go straight to a level that would have his workshop steamy from the friction between them. Because it wasn't only awkward tension he felt simmering between them.

Oh, no.

Hot, sexual tension had been floating back and forth since the moment he laid eyes on her.

She had terrible taste in men.

Well, not anymore.

He was about to prove to her just how much he was the best thing that had ever entered her life.

3

HOPE ADJUSTED the cream-colored hat that she found at a craft fair this past summer. There had been vendors galore at the fair, from homemade honey to artwork to fresh baked bread—it was hard not to buy at least three loaves. Her scarf and knit mittens matched. Sometimes she liked to match. Sometimes she liked to wear the most outrageous things. It all depended on her mood at the time.

Tonight, she wanted to dress to impress.

She shoved the zipper up on her slick winter coat another inch until it hit the end. Not that it mattered. There were like five steps to make before she'd be in a warm building taking the dumb thing off.

Nerves were hitting her like a freight train hitting a wall at max speed.

She never got nervous with a guy. Flirting came easy, as if it were a natural trait she was born with. It wasn't like learning to knit, which, quite frankly, was impossible to do. She didn't understand the mechanics of it. Loop this way, loop that way, under, over. Too intricate for her. Yet she watched her sister do it as if it were nothing more than tying her shoelaces together.

Maybe she was nervous because she wanted this to work out—more than she cared to admit.

Mase was a good guy. She didn't have to doubt herself for once. Stu thought he was decent. Chasity as well. Even the chief of police. There wasn't a better reference than the chief of police himself, one of the nicest men in town.

That's why she knew it would all fall apart eventually. She didn't date the good guys. Bad boys were more her thing. Or finding out after having great sex just how much of a loser the guy really was—that was more her forte.

She didn't know where to begin dating a good guy.

Well, a knock was a good start.

She rapped twice on the door before taking a step back and looking around. Mase had texted her to meet him in his workshop behind the house. A small shoveled path led from his driveway alongside his house to the back. Enough room to walk comfortably, especially if he carried wood back and forth from here. His house looked small but big enough for a bachelor. One- or two-bedroom house if she had to guess. It was dark out, but the yard appeared small. Not much could be seen other than a large tree near the opposite side of the house.

The workshop was big. Almost as big as the house. She imagined he spent a lot of time out here. He had a string of icicle lights hanging from the gutter, as he did in front of the house as well. A wired, lit-up snowman stood close to the door as well. He wore a goofy face with a broomstick in his hand. The merry song immediately popped in her head, and she chuckled as she stared at the yard ornament.

The door swung open.

"I missed the joke." His grin widened as they stared at each other.

"Your snowman is adorable."

He peeked his head out, his lips curling up even more. "Found it on the side of the road. Shocked it even worked when I plugged it in. But hey, I wasn't going to let him sit all alone out there. Now he has a home."

He tossed his head toward the inside. "Come on. It's cold out."

The warmth hit her as soon as she walked inside. It was heavenly and oh so sweet compared to the brutal cold outside.

He had a decent-size furnace to her right, which obviously did a great job heating the place. A small woodbox sat next to it, filled to the rim with wood. She didn't see a woodpile gathered outside, so she wondered where he kept the rest.

Not that he didn't have wood anywhere else. The entire building was filled with wood of all kinds, in every corner. There was a long workbench to the left with tools galore. He had two large tables in the middle where he created his magic. She could see half of the frame for the manger already completed.

"Have you even stopped to breathe today?" she asked with a laugh as she moved closer to the table.

"For a minute or two."

His laughter in return filled her heart with joy—and a bit of trepidation. Flirting was her jam, yet she didn't know what to say or do. The last thing she wanted to do was say the wrong thing and get booted out. She wouldn't blame him. She hadn't exactly given him the right signals. More like criss-crossed and mismatched the entire time since she first met him.

"I'll take your jacket. You'll start sweating to death any minute."

That was no lie. She was already feeling the heat spread under her armpits. He had a great furnace. It did its job and then some.

She unzipped her jacket, pulled off her mittens and hat, shoving the items in the pockets, and then handed it to him, feeling self-conscious the entire time. She didn't miss the way he looked her over.

She had opted for jeans—her ass looked great in them —with a white sweater. Nothing fancy. Nothing that said she wasn't interested, but also nothing that said 'do me now.' She had tried for a middle ground kind of outfit. She unwrapped her scarf and set it on the workbench.

"Nice workshop. It's...cozy."

He had a wooden coat rack hanging in the corner near the door. She wondered if he made it himself. His eyes twinkled as he neared her once again.

"Thanks. I practically live in here more than my house. I love being in here."

A small couch sat in the back with a twenty-inch TV on a short stand. That told her he wasn't fibbing. There was even a small fridge near a counter in the back where a sink was. All this place needed was a bed and he could call this his house.

"So, how was your day?"

His simple question, like asking about the weather, put her at ease a little bit. It told her he was as nervous as her.

"Same day as yesterday. Work at the church and then go home. My life is pretty boring."

Ugh. Why did she say that? She did not need to add that last bit.

"And you? You've been busy."

He nodded. "Got the frame done. I stopped at Diana's Diner and put some shelves up. They've been wanting to upgrade for a while, and the one shelf broke last week, so it moved their timeline up a bit. Then I came home and started on the manger."

Now she felt bad. Imposing on his time.

"You didn't even eat?"

"Oh, no, Tara made me a sandwich. I scarfed it down on the way home. Did you?"

She nodded. Leftover lasagna she made like a month ago and froze. Although, one of Tara's sandwiches sounded good. Tara had owned Diana's Diner for as long as she could remember. Nobody could make a Ruben sandwich like her.

"Thanks for working so hard and so quickly on the Nativity set. Father Benson was so upset by what happened."

"Of course. I didn't mind when Chief Duncan called. Can't believe whoever hit it just left. Jackass."

She chuckled and took a seat on one of the stools near the workbench where the manger sat.

"Well, they won't be getting any goodies in their stocking this year, that's for sure."

Mase joined her in laughing, then pointed at the manger. "Mind if I work while we chat. There is beer in the fridge if you want to grab one."

"Sure. You want one, too?" She stood up. "And please, work. I don't have to stay long."

"Yeah, I'll take one."

She headed for the fridge.

"I don't want you leaving any time soon."

She nearly tripped in her steps.

"Is it getting hot in here?"

Her heart pounded by his last question. Because, oh,

yeah, the heat was starting to turn up all right. She plucked two beers from the fridge and walked back toward him with a bit more confidence than she walked in with.

She set his bottle near him, popped hers open, and took a long swig.

"I think it's just starting to heat up."

His intense gaze skewered her to the bone. Not in a bad way either. Those tingles of bliss she had on the drive here exploded into full-blown desire. She wanted this man. Had since the moment she laid eyes on him. If the way his gaze honed in on her like a heat-seeking missile was any indication, he felt the same way.

His hand clasped her waist as the other one wound around her neck. He pulled her closer.

"You're the most beautiful woman I've ever met."

She highly doubted that.

Then his lips met hers and all thought was lost.

This man could kiss.

If she didn't watch herself, he would steal her heart before she had a chance to lock it up.

Oh, wait. He had already stolen it, except she had a hard time accepting it.

WERE THINGS MOVING TOO FAST? Were they about to do something they should wait on? As she opened her mouth and he moved the kiss to newer heights, he didn't care how fast they moved.

He'd wanted this woman from the moment he laid eyes on her, and he was going to have her. She was in his arms, and he never wanted her to leave.

His fingers tightened on her neck as he pulled her closer. The cold beer bottle still in her hand barely penetrated his thoughts. When a bit of the liquid trickled out when she tipped it, that got his attention.

The kiss slowed down, and the needy groan that fell from her lips as he pulled away told him all he needed to know.

She wanted what was about to happen as much as him.

"Let me take that." He grabbed the bottle and set it next to his.

Before she could say anything else, his lips were back on hers and he was hoisting her up. Her legs wrapped around his waist, his cock begging for more. For the clothes to disappear.

He knew his workshop inside and out. Where everything was located, right down to his last tool. As he made his way from the table to the couch against the back wall, he didn't bump or knock into anything. He set her down on the couch gently, hardly moving his lips from hers.

"I'm going to have you naked in about five seconds flat, unless you tell me no."

Her teeth grazed her bottom lip, a sly smirk hiding. "One, two..."

He didn't wait for her to finish counting. Her sweater disappeared, revealing a white lacy bra underneath. He took about half a second to appreciate it before unclasping it and removing it altogether. His mouth couldn't stop itself, attaching to one of her nipples and sucking hard. Her entire body arched off the couch at the touch.

His hands made their way to her jeans as he continued to give her beautiful breasts the attention they deserved. Sucking, nipping, and devouring as if he'd never get another chance to do it again. And shit, what did he know? Maybe he wouldn't. Maybe she was only giving him this night, and then she'd disappear once again.

Nope. He wouldn't think bad thoughts. Only sweet, desirable thoughts were permitted at the moment.

Her pants and matching lacy panties were gone within another few seconds, along with her cute brown boots she wore.

She put a hand to his chest before he could finish the love he had been giving her with his mouth.

"Naked, now." Then her gaze traveled up and down his length, glittering with anticipation.

He chuckled and stood up, removing his clothes with a speed he normally didn't have. He didn't want to waste a moment of this with her. He dug out a condom from his wallet and then covered his body with hers.

"I've been dying to get you in my arms since the moment I laid eyes on you."

She jerked, a slight frown appearing before it vanished as if it never happened. He decided to ignore it. His words scared her. Perhaps no other man had ever said such sweet things to her before.

Well, he wasn't just some guy.

If she let him, he'd prove he was *the* guy for her.

Then his mouth was back on hers and his hands started exploring. Weaving up and down the length of her a few times before settling in her most intimate spot that was already wet and ready for him.

But teasing was fun, so he did.

Circling his finger in a rhythmic pattern that had her arching her body this way and that, a low, needy groan filtered between their kisses.

She bit his lip when an orgasm erupted from her.

Boy, that was quick, and not what he expected from her. His lip throbbed until she swiped a tongue across it.

"Sorry, I don't know what came over me."

By the daring twinkle in her eye, she knew exactly what she had done. He didn't mind the pain. It was an erotic sort of pain he had never experienced before. It told him she had enjoyed every second of it.

"Let's see how many times I can make you come tonight."

Her eyes lit up with pleasure as her hands grabbed his ass and squeezed.

"Oh, challenge accepted."

Another chuckle released as he tore open the condom package and slid it on. In the next move, he was deep inside her.

She felt so damn good.

More than his dreams had ever conjured.

The pace started slow and easy. Her hands wove up and down his back. As the pace slowly increased, so did her motions, her nails dragging instead of soothing.

Each touch, each movement from her urged him on.

Faster. Deeper. Stronger.

She started peppering small kisses on his neck, which only skyrocketed his desire even further.

"Hold on, sweetheart."

He gripped her hips and thrust harder. So fiercely that she wouldn't be able to deny how he felt. She'd run screaming from his arms if he told her he loved her already.

How could he love a woman so quickly? So deeply? Hell, even he didn't know. He just did.

Now that he knew how delicious she tasted, how glorious it felt to be with her, he wasn't giving up on them.

Because he had an inkling she wasn't going to make it easy on him.

"Oh, Mase. Yes."

Her whispered words had him increasing the pace even more. Thrust after thrust until he couldn't hold back.

He pumped hard one last time before an intense bliss settled over him.

"Oh, so close," she whimpered.

Oh, hell, no. He wasn't about to leave her hanging.

With the ecstasy still flowing through him—and all he wanted to do was bask in the glory—he found her sweet spot and started rubbing, coaxing another beautiful moan from her. It didn't take long for another wondrous orgasm to escape from her.

He kissed her, unable to hold off the triumphant smile on his face. "That's two."

"The most I've had in a night is four."

Well, damn. That was being honest. Not that he wanted to know what another guy had done to her.

But he wasn't one to be beat.

"Then you bet your ass it'll be five tonight."

The delicious grin on her lips had him kissing her until that adorable, needy moan she could produce erupted once more.

They had all night, though. He wouldn't elicit another one from her so soon.

He ended the kiss before getting up, plucked the condom off, and tossed it in the trash. He cleaned himself near the sink and then turned to her where she still laid on the couch looking sated and gorgeous as hell. Her red hair was fanned out on the cushion. Her cheeks flushed from an intense lovemaking he had never done. Her lips were still spread into a sly grin, as if waiting for more right. This. Second.

Still naked, and not at all self-conscious about it, he grabbed their beers and walked back to the couch. He lifted her legs and sat down, resting them on top of his lap. Then he set her beer on her stomach, which had her gasping and giggling at the coldness.

"Naughty. But thank you." She took the beer and a sip, a bit of it dribbling down her chin, considering she didn't sit up all the way to take a drink.

He leaned down and licked the liquid off. "I think that might be my new way of drinking."

"Kind of messy."

"But sexy as hell."

Then he poured a small amount on her stomach, eliciting another sharp gasp. His lips attacked her luscious skin, licking and soaking up the beer. Her gasp turned quickly into a delightful moan.

Before he could do it again, she put a hand on the bottle.

"You'll ruin your couch. It'll stink like beer forever."

He shrugged. "But it'll make me think of you. Lying here naked, looking gorgeous as hell."

Her leg started to rub his cock, making it jump to attention. It'd been a while since he'd seen any action; he wasn't about to ignore it.

"You make me feel sexy."

He wasn't sure how to respond to that because he never imagined Hope didn't know how attractive she was.

"Because you are sexy."

Words sometimes weren't enough. He moved until he was between her legs. She eyed him, her brows pleated as if wondering what he was about to do. Pour more beer on her? Another round of sweaty sex? Because, besides the fire roaring in the corner, things were really heating up in the joint.

He winked before his mouth found what it craved. A taste of her. Still wet and ready for him.

Number three was about to happen. While he had fun lapping up her juices and making her come once again, he'd think about how number four and five would go.

Because she wasn't leaving until he made his goal.

4

"Oh, this sweater has to be my fave. Better than yesterday."

Hope took a seat on a stool as Theresa filled up a to-go coffee cup for her. She didn't always stop in for a coffee before work, but when she did, Theresa just knew. She glanced at her sweater and chuckled, the little bit a person could see since she didn't zip up her coat all the way was funny.

A dancing camel and llama were rocking around a Christmas tree. There were two buttons that made the sweater even better. She had hit one of them, lighting the tree. She pushed the other button.

Theresa snorted, nearly dropping the coffee.

The lights started to flash as music filled the air, showcasing how the animals were rocking around the tree.

"Yep. Definitely better than yesterday." Theresa set the coffee cup in front of her, still giggling.

Yesterday she wore a red-and-white sweater with Santa on it sitting in his sleigh. It was pretty boring and tame compared to the other Santa sweater she had in the closet.

That one said 'where my ho's at?', but she didn't think that would be appropriate to wear inside a church.

"Thank you. I've been dying for this cup of java." She took a sip and relished in the slight muddy flavor that slid down her throat. Theresa, bless her heart, always made terrible coffee, and Hope, for one, loved every sip. Because she tried. It was made with love.

Theresa rolled her eyes, knowing how everyone felt about her coffee. "The new Nativity scene looks amazing. I can't believe how fast Mase built it."

Neither could Hope, but when that man put his mind to something, he got shit done.

Like last week when he insisted she come five times before he'd let her leave. She actually came six, and every single one had blown her mind. There wasn't an inch of that place their lovemaking didn't touch. It'd be impossible for him to work in there and not think of her.

"He has magic in his hands."

Theresa snorted again, her eyes dancing with laughter.

Yeah, probably the wrong thing to say, considering they'd been hanging out the past week—every single day. It wouldn't be hard to decipher what that could also mean. The entire town knew they were a thing. A couple? Together? In a relationship?

Hope didn't want to label it. For now, she'd say they were a *thing*.

"I bet he does."

"Whatever. You're married. Stop looking at other men."

Theresa put a hand over her belly, rubbing, as she stared lovingly at the bump. It had taken them over three years to get pregnant. She hung out with Theresa on occasion, as did Chasity. She didn't know all the details, only that she and Aiden had tried so many times to get pregnant that they finally decided to try in-vitro fertilization. They were due in April with twins on the way. At least one girl, but the other little stinker wouldn't move in the right position and they weren't able to tell the sex of that baby. Either way, the soon-to-be parents were over the moon welcoming two beautiful babies into the world.

Theresa looked up at her, smiling. "I hear Mase's brother is coming for Christmas. Are you all getting together?"

Ugh. Hope didn't want to think about it. Mase casually mentioned his brother coming, but didn't come right out and ask her about Christmas Day plans. She wasn't excited one bit for the Christmas Chasity had planned. The last thing she wanted to do was be in the same room as Mayor Hafferty. Or ruin Christmas because she had a sour attitude about the guy. Fine, if he was trying to change his ways, that was great. But she didn't believe it for one minute.

"Not sure yet. We haven't talked about it much."

Theresa's eyes widened. "Christmas is in less than a week. You've been spending every day with him. Don't you think you should talk about it?"

"It's not a big deal."

Theresa sighed and shook her head. "You're hopeless, Hope."

"You don't see the irony in that," she said, cocking a brow. She *was* hopeless. Having great sex every day wasn't going to stop the chaos from wreaking havoc inside her.

If anything, it was increasing it. Confusing her more. Testing her patience and her emotions to the brink.

"What I see is a friend...lost." Theresa reached out and touched her hand. "I'm always here for you."

Wow. What a good way to describe her. Lost. Yeah, she had felt that way the past year. Floating around, every day doing mundane things because it was required of her, but she did feel lost. Maybe a little broken, too.

"We're doing a Secret Santa thing at work. Can you wrap up one of your necklaces for me? Oh, and a bracelet."

Theresa sighed again, frustrated at Hope for ignoring her concern. She headed to the other end of the counter where a display of her jewelry sat for customers to buy. Theresa also took special orders, but not as much this year. Hope figured it had something to do with her pregnancy and not being up to full power. While she was joking and laughing with her, Theresa looked tired, dark circles under her eyes. A few times she had put her hand on her belly, but she had also put a hand on her back as if that were bothering her.

She boxed up the jewelry, wrapping it in green tissue paper and placing it in a white box with a red bow on top.

Hope put forty bucks on the counter and waved off Theresa when she started to move toward the register to grab change.

"Keep the tip. Have a good day."

"Thank you. You shouldn't, but I'm too tired to argue with you."

"Don't work too hard."

Then Hope waved good-bye and headed outside into the cold. Not as bad as last week, but still cold. She hopped in her car and drove the short distance to the church, greeting Father Benson on the way to her office.

Her phone pinged as soon as she sat down.

Mase: Dinner tonight?

I thought your brother flew in today.

Mase: He does.

So he was suggesting dinner with his brother? Hope didn't know about that.

That made what was happening between them sound serious. They weren't serious. They were just having fun. Great, amazing sex.

Hope wasn't ready for a real relationship. After deciding to give Mase a chance—because he was a nice guy—life seemed on a more even keel.

But meeting the family already? She thought they'd ease into something. Whatever that something might be.

Bottom line, she couldn't trust her judgment. She always made the wrong call. Despite everyone singing Mase's praises, she wanted to take it slow. Meeting the family wasn't taking anything slow.

Sorry. Can't tonight. Have plans with my sister.

Lying left a nasty taste in her mouth, her gut swirling with unease, but it had to be done. She wasn't ready to meet his brother.

She might never be ready. Every time she tried to envision herself married with kids, living together in a cozy house with a ridiculous white picket fence, the image blurred. It was never focused.

Because it would never happen.

Mase was a good guy.

She was chaos walking, and he'd eventually get sick of that.

She'd enjoy the sex while she could, but she wasn't banking on a forever kind of relationship developing between them.

"I SET up an air mattress in my spare room." Mase winced. "Sorry, I don't use it as a bedroom. It's more for storage and crap. But I moved it all so there's plenty of room for you two."

"It's all good, bro." Jaxson smiled as if he meant it.

Mia, on the other hand, looked concerned. Her brows pleated, yet her lips turned upward as if she were forcing a smile out.

He didn't know his brother's fiancée well. He'd met her here and there when he visited New York to see his brother. She and Jaxson had been friends for a long time before they became a couple, but generally, when he visited Jaxson, he didn't see her much. The last time he did go see his brother —their relationship had just started to blossom—he never laid eyes on her.

So it was hard to get a read on her.

His house was on the smaller side, but he bought it with his own hard-earned money and he was damn proud of that. He might have his buddies over now and again, but they were all bachelors like him.

His eyes glided around his small living room, trying to envision it with the eyes of a woman. It was neat and put together. Decent-sized couch, with a large fifty-five-inch TV hanging on the wall. A bookshelf filled with movies. He wasn't a reading sort of guy. No clutter. The kitchen was the same. Dishes washed and put away—most nights. Upstairs had two rooms and a full bath. Sometimes it sucked having to rush upstairs when he needed to go to the bathroom, but a person did what they had to do when they only had one bathroom.

It wasn't a bad house.

It was just small.

Now he was curious what Hope would think of it. The past week had been amazing. They'd been inseparable. Some nights he went to her place. The other nights she came over here to his workshop. They never ventured into his house. He'd have to rectify that the next time she came over. He was falling hard and fast for the woman, so he needed to get a read on what she thought of his house. It wouldn't be a make and break kind of deal, but he needed to prepare for any possible scenario.

"You have a lovely house," Mia finally said.

Her smile appeared real this time, so Mase took it that she wasn't lying. So maybe Hope would think the same thing.

He wished she were here.

Although he wouldn't bet all his money on it, he swore she lied to him today about having plans with her sister. She had never mentioned it last night—not that she had to tell him every little thing—but it felt...off when he read the text.

"Thanks. I'm happy with it. I spend most of my time in my workshop, though."

"Let me bring the suitcases upstairs, then what's on the agenda?" Jaxson asked as he grabbed two of the three suitcases.

"Whatever you feel like. I have no special plans planned." He chuckled, looking between the two. Was he supposed to plan stuff? Normally, when his brother visited, they did whatever. Hung out, chilled, and caught up on each other's life. Maybe with Mia in the mix he was supposed to make an itinerary.

Shit. He should've asked Hope's opinion. But he sensed he shouldn't rush things with her. Talking about his brother always gave him a feeling that she didn't like those conversations much—at least the ones about him visiting.

Yeah, something was off with her today. He knew deep in the pit of his stomach she had feigned plans to get out of meeting his brother. It scared her for some reason.

He managed to get caught up on all projects he and Cam were working on, so he had off through to the twenty-seventh. His time would be devoted to his brother. No matter what was going on, they usually tried to get together for a major holiday. Since they didn't get together any other time this past year, Christmas won. His quick trip to New York this past summer didn't count. That was more of an apology trip because they had been having a few spats that he didn't like having with his brother. Things were good now.

"Well, I'll put the presents under the tree and we can chat about it." Mia grabbed the other suitcase and rolled it over to his tree sitting in front of the small bay window.

He rushed over and plugged it in. It didn't even occur to him to plug it in. He almost didn't get a tree, since he rarely hung out in his living room, but since Jaxson was coming, he figured he should.

It was pathetic looking. White lights wove around it with a handful of ornaments. Not much hung on the limbs. But the lights made it pretty.

"My favorite. White lights." Mia's smile brightened even further since she had walked in.

Then she set the suitcase on its side and unzipped it.

Mase couldn't hold in his laughter. "Whoa. You guys weren't playing. That entire suitcase is full of presents. It's only us three."

Mia shrugged, though her eyes twinkled with delight. "I

love Christmas. Buying presents is fun. I might've gone over-board. I hope you like everything."

"I have no doubt I will."

He was easy to please. Give him a bag of peanuts and he'd be in heaven. Cashews, specifically. He found out that Hope was easy to please as well. She loved black licorice. He made sure to have a full jar in his workshop this past week just for her. Her eyes always lit up so magically when she saw it filled to the brim every single time. If only he could keep that wonderful look in her eyes all the time.

"Want a drink?"

Mia paused, her hand on a present covered with penguins wearing a Santa hat wrapping paper. "Sure. Thanks."

Mase tossed a hand toward the coffee table. "I bought your favorite. White chocolate-covered pretzels. There are a few more bags in the pantry, so help yourself. You're welcome to anything here."

"Thanks, Mase. That was kind of you."

This time he shrugged. "It's what family does. You'll be my sis in no time."

He couldn't remember the exact date they picked, but it was sometime in September. Jaxson had said something about it not being too hot, yet not too cold. He figured that was more of Mia's concern rather than Jaxson's.

"It means more than I can say. Thank you." Her eyes glistened with unshed tears.

Mase knew she had it rough growing up. Bastard of a father. Mother died of cancer. Ended up killing her father in self-defense. Yeah, rough didn't begin to describe it. But he meant what he said. Jaxson loved her, then so did he. Family was everything.

"Beer or wine?"

She laughed. "Surprise me. It's been a crazy past few months, and I'm ready to relax and have fun."

"You got it."

He grabbed three beers because it was easier than opening a bottle of wine and walked back into the living room. Jaxson was by the tree with Mia. It was full of presents underneath it.

"Well, shit. My measly presents fail in comparison. I'll grab them from the closet and add them."

"Dude, it's about the spirit of giving."

He rolled his eyes at Jaxson, knowing quite well how full of shit his brother was. When they were growing up, they counted down to the last present to make sure it was fair. That they both got the same amount. Sometimes they'd even argue over who got what. Jealous of each other's toys.

But, Mase figured, as adults, it could be seen as that. The spirit of giving. Still, the two presents—for each of them—would not be enough. He'd have to grab another two, at least, so he didn't look pathetic.

"So when do we get to meet Hope?"

Although the question was asked in a friendly manner, Mase heard the underlying tension. Jaxson still wasn't a fan of her. Not after he told Jaxson she was married when he first met her, even though that had turned out not to be true.

"Plans with her sister tonight. Hopefully tomorrow."

If she didn't suddenly create plans with her sister again. He still had an inkling she lied to him.

"How was your flight?" A conversation change was needed. He didn't want to talk about Hope, at least not yet.

Jaxson took a seat on the couch. Mia joined him. He decided to stay standing as the couch wasn't that huge and he didn't want to strain his neck looking at his brother from the side.

"Uneventful. Long. I'm starving. Did you throw anything in the crockpot?"

He knew how much Mase loved his crockpot meals. After working a long day, it was easier to have his meal already prepared for him. He wasn't a fan of frozen meals.

Of course, the one day he should, he didn't. He worked all day getting his house ready for these two, then the long drive to pick them up from the airport. He ran out of time.

"Shit. No." Mase laughed, then took a sip of beer. "We can go eat out somewhere."

"Nothing too fancy. We're starving."

Jaxson knew there was nothing that fancy around these parts, anyway. Only small towns dotted around with lots of countryside.

"And alcohol. It's gotta have that." Mia took a long pull of her beer, emptying half of it.

Mase chuckled. "I know the perfect place."

With any luck, Hope would be there with her sister.

"WHEN IS Chasity getting off of work?" Hope asked as Stu grabbed a beer for Drew, one of the regulars.

Stu grinned. "Not until late tonight. She picked up an extra shift to help out Adam. His sister is almost due, and he wants to be there for her since the baby's father up and ran out. Asshole."

Yeah, Hope could agree with that assessment. Evelyn was a sweetheart, a little naive at times, but one of the sweetest people in town. Evelyn didn't like it, but some people loved to call her Eve for short, considering her brother's name was Adam. Way too many kids loved to tease her about it in school. Hope, even though she'd been two grades ahead, had always stuck up for her when she could. Unfortunately, she hooked up with the wrong loser, got pregnant, and now was on her own to raise a baby.

Well, not completely alone. She had a great brother willing to be there for her—for everything.

It was just as well her lie would fall apart. She should've never told Mase to begin with that she had plans with her sister. She didn't know her sister's schedule by heart, and it had been a fifty-fifty chance she'd be off. She got nabbed with the wrong fifty percent.

"I figured you'd be hanging out with Mase."

"His brother came into town today from New York. Family time, you know."

Stu nodded, as if that made sense. "I'm surprised he didn't ask you to join them."

She didn't wince, but her face must've displayed her oh-shit moment anyhow.

Laughter floated around her. "Ah, so he did ask. And you're looking for Chasity for a completely different reason other than wanting to hang out."

"Things are moving fast. I mean, meeting the family already?" Hope shivered. She was so not ready for it.

Stu looked behind her shoulder as the bell above the door jingled—a new add by Chasity for the holiday spirit. It sounded merry she had said. A wily grin spread across his face.

"Well, too fast or not, you're about to meet them."

Her heart sped up, her eyes rounding in shock.

"In my experience, it's better to tell the truth than run away from the fear inside."

"Whatever, Stu. I don't want your damn pep talk."

Although she sounded surly about it, she appreciated that he cared.

He knew she was only being grouchy with what was about to happen because he chuckled and winked, then said hello to Mase.

"What can I get you?"

She decided to be a wimp and not turn toward Mase yet. Let them get their drinks ordered first and then maybe she'd have the gumption to face him since she lied.

"Menu first and I guess a few beers. This is my brother Jaxson and his fiancée, Mia." Mase pointed toward Stu. "This is Stu. He owns Hafferty's Bar. Best place in town to get nachos and a good beer."

"Oh, man, you should try the pretzels, too. Lynn's been making me fresh dough for them. Whoa! That woman knows how to bake." Stu reached out and shook Jaxson and Mia's hand, returning their greetings

Shit.

Her time was up. She had to face the consequences.

She turned slightly in her chair and came face-to-face with Mase. He wore a short smile, yet she saw the pain in his eyes. He knew she lied.

"Chasity in the bathroom?"

She swallowed, hoping to clear the sudden dryness in her throat. "She had to pick up a shift for a co-worker. His sister is almost due. Poor baby. Nobody should have their birthday so close to Christmas. You get so robbed of presents."

Her laughter sounded forced, yet she had to keep her cool. Displaying nonchalance and like she didn't create a huge gap between them was the key.

Silence permeated the air. Not just between them, but Jaxson and Mia as well.

Stu set the menus on the bar, then grabbed three beers.

That was the only noise—besides the other patrons in the establishment—that circled them.

"Well, wave a hand at me when you're ready to order. Pretty slow night, so it shouldn't take too long to cook anything."

Then Stu walked away.

Mase released a heavy breath, then brightened his smile before stepping more toward her side and turning around to his brother.

"Jaxson, I'd like you to meet the woman I'm always raving about. This is Hope. And, Hope, this is my brother Jaxson and his fiancée, Mia."

Hope stood up and shook hands as Stu had. Of course, her hands probably felt clammier and shakier than Stu's. She had years to perfect how to put on a good front working for the mayor. Despite the nerves running through her veins, she maintained a jovial attitude.

"It's nice to finally meet you, Hope." Jaxson stared at her with a gentle smile, yet she saw the wariness and distrust in his gaze. "Is your sister here, too?"

Oh, yeah. Definitely distrust. He sounded like Mase, hoping to weed out her lie right this second.

"She had to work tonight."

"I'm sorry to hear that. Would you like to join us?" Mia asked.

Out of all of them, her smile wasn't forced. It was bright and beautiful and filled with kindness. As if she sensed the tension lingering in the air and wanted to evaporate it as best as she could.

"Sure. Of course."

"We'll go grab a table."

Then Jaxson and Mia walked away as if sensing they needed a moment alone.

"Did I do something wrong?" The hurt in his tone gutted her.

"No, why would you think that?" Of course, admitting her mistake wasn't going to come that easy, even if she felt terrible about it.

He picked up one of her hands. "You lied to me. You never had plans with your sister."

She stared at their hands where he was drawing small circles over the top of hers with his thumb. Soft, soothing circles as if she were a frightened animal and needed to be calmed down. Maybe that held a ring of truth.

"Mase..." She cleared her throat, this time from the invisible force clogging it. "Meeting the family seems..."

He lifted her hand and pressed a kiss to it. "It doesn't matter what it might've seemed like. It's done. You met them."

She looked at him. "You don't think things are moving too fast."

A sultry grin lit up his features. "If I say what I want to say, you'll be moving fast—right out the door."

Oh, she could only imagine what this man was thinking. She saw his looks. The heat in his eyes. The desire. The... love? She tried to ignore what she was seeing.

It was too soon.

She wasn't ready for any of that. Sure, she might have a small inkling of love in her heart for him, but could she trust it? Could she trust him? She was always leading herself down the wrong path; she didn't want to make the same mistakes again.

"Look, we can take this at your pace. What makes you happy makes me happy. Just..." His smile disappeared as the ache centered in his eyes once again. "Don't lie to me. Please, don't do that again."

"Okay. I'm sorry. I never meant to hurt you. I panicked at the thought of meeting your brother. I really am sorry."

He leaned forward and kissed her. His touch, as always, lit her body on fire. She wanted more. Even though they were in a bar, she wasn't opposed to taking him to the bathroom and having her dirty way with him in a stall.

That's what he did to her. With one simple kiss.

Made her lose her mind. Excited her senses. Drove her wild.

"Come on. Jaxson's a good guy and Mia is sweet. Shy and quiet until you get to know her."

Hope didn't argue when Mase intertwined their fingers together. She grabbed her fruity drink before walking with him toward the table in the corner they had picked out.

"I don't think your brother likes me."

Mase paused, then said, "Of course he does."

But his moment of hesitation told Hope everything she needed to know.

Mase knew how to lie, too.

It didn't make it right, but she supposed she deserved it after lying to him more than once.

They ordered food. Hope did, too. A small appetizer platter because hearing them chat about food made her hungry as well.

Conversation flowed as Jaxson and Mia talked about their wedding plans, as well as their good friends, Gabby and Dane, getting married. The entire talk gave her the heebie-jeebies. Not a topic she wanted to discuss. Yet she couldn't say so and ruin the mood. She smiled and nodded when appropriate and nearly kissed Mia on the lips when she finally changed it.

"So, what do you do, Hope?"

Fair question as Mase had mentioned before the

wedding conversation that Jaxson was a detective with the NYPD and Mia worked at a local theater on Off-Broadway. Both amazing professions. She felt so lame and ridiculous compared to the three of them. Even Mase had a successful, wonderful business that he owned.

"I work at the church in town as the secretary."

It sounded even more pathetic saying it out loud.

"Oh, how wonderful. I loved going to church with my mother when she was alive. It was the only time I felt truly peaceful." Mia had a sad, wistful look on her face. "Of course, Christmastime was always so magical. The decorations, the music, the wondrous spirit in the air."

"I never knew that. I feel like I should've known this. We can go to church together," Jaxson said, placing a hand over Mia's.

"That's sweet of you. Our busy schedules don't always mesh."

"I'll make them mesh."

Wow.

Hope knew Chasity and Stu had a great relationship, but this moment between Jaxson and Mia knocked any moment Chasity and Stu might've had out of the park. The love in his eyes, the devotion in his tone was beyond anything she had ever heard before.

It made her wish for the same thing.

Mase didn't touch her in any way, but she still felt his presence wrap around her, cocooning her in a warm embrace. As if silently telling her he could give her the same thing.

"I'd really like that."

"Then it's done." Jaxson sealed it with a kiss.

"The church is putting on a fun little event for the kids in town tomorrow. We could use a few more volunteers if you want to help. I mean, you probably have plans. Forget I said anything."

How dumb. Like they wanted to hang out with her at her work, especially with a bunch of rambunctious kids.

Just because she saw a magical moment didn't mean she could hold onto it. Although she wanted to.

"That sounds like a great idea." Mia didn't even look at the men for confirmation. She said it, so it was decided.

This time, Mase reached under the table and grabbed her hand from her lap and squeezed. She wasn't sure why or what it meant, but she tightened her grip in return.

Perhaps meeting his family wasn't so bad after all.

5

"Seriously, you guys didn't have to come with." Although, Mase was glad they had.

He wanted to spend time with his brother, but he wanted to spend as much time as he could with Hope. He had had a strong inkling she lied to him, and he hated how right he had been. She was scared. He got it. They were moving kind of fast in their relationship. Of course, he sensed she wouldn't like it if he called what they had a relationship.

But hell, he didn't want to share her with anyone. He'd have to have a talk with her and put some sort of label on what they were. The last thing he wanted was some other guy putting hands on her. She was his. Nobody else's.

"This sounds like so much fun. I can't wait." Mia rubbed her hands gleefully—and probably to stave off the cold.

It was single digits, and the wind hit him in the face with a sharp bite. He was grateful this event wasn't an outdoor one.

Jaxson opened the door near the back of the church, letting Mia enter first. He followed behind his brother. He heard the chatter before he saw anyone. As soon as they walked a few feet down the hallway, they came upon a set of doors propped open. Inside was a flurry of people. Of course, the parking lot outside told him it would be a busy event.

Small tables were set up around the room with a long table toward the back where refreshments were set up. Doughnuts, croissants, and pastries galore. Most likely provided by Lynn's Sweet Treat Delights. She made the best goodies. A coffee pot with white mugs sat ready to warm people up. There was another table set up for hot chocolate. There were small bags filled with hot cocoa, marshmallows, and crushed candy canes waiting to be consumed. Kids were everywhere in the room. Some eating yummy treats or making their own hot chocolate. Others were at the small tables making crafts.

"Hey, you made it." Hope appeared out of nowhere looking adorable in an elf outfit. Green from head to toe with a cute green pointy hat and even an added effect to her ears to make them pointy as well.

"You are so cute." Then he kissed her before she could protest or back away.

She grinned before pulling out Santa hats from behind her back. She plopped one on his head.

"Now you look just as cute." She turned to Jaxson and Mia. "I have one more Santa hat or there are other things on that table over there." She pointed to another table he hadn't seen against the wall to the right.

It looked like a station for dressing up as a Santa, elf, reindeer, or a snowman. The carrots with the strings attached looked interesting. The black top hats look fun, but no thanks to putting a carrot over his nose.

"How fun. Thank you for inviting us," Mia said, taking

the extra hat from her and putting it on Jaxson's head. "I'll think I'll be an elf like Hope."

"Get your accessory and then pick a table. Each table has a surprise bag filled with Christmas crafts. Fun ornaments for the kids to decorate either with stickers, paint, gluing pompoms, and so many other things. Some kids will need help, but not all of them." Hope picked up a bag from one of the tables near them. "See. All the supplies are in the bag, except for the glue or the paint and stuff. But it's all on the table. If you need something you don't see, find me."

Mia took the bag, smiling. "Oh, how adorable. Look at the saying."

Mase nodded and smiled, almost mirroring his brother's expression. All the bags had different holiday expressions on them. The one Mia held said 'Tidings and Joy.' The other bags said 'Merry and Bright,' 'Snow Much Fun,' 'Happy Hollydays,' 'Peppermint Sweet,' and 'Holiday Cheer.' If a person wasn't in the holiday mood, this would be sure to do it.

"I'm going to grab an elf hat." Mia walked away with Jaxson following.

Mase figured Jaxson wanted to stay close to Mia, since he hadn't been completely thrilled to come today. But he did because Mia was excited by the prospect. No doubt his brother walked away to also give him time alone with Hope.

"So, what can I do to help?"

Hope's lips curled up into a sultry grin. "Weren't you listening? Naughty, naughty. I said to pick a table."

Mase laughed. He could do naughty if she wanted him to. "Well, yeah, I heard that."

He glanced around, slight nerves suddenly attacking him. He didn't exactly know how to do crafts. Sure, he built things, but not these kinds of things. Tiny as shit pieces of art, like googly eyes and small scraps of paper. His big fingers wouldn't attach anything correctly.

Hope drew closer and ran a hand down his chest before practically jumping back as if the hand of God pushed her back. No naughty business in church.

"You're nervous."

He chuckled. "I'm not exactly an arts and crafts kind of guy."

"Yeah, well, you are a crafty guy. You make magic with your hands." Her eyes sparkled with heat, telling him she wasn't only talking about the things he made with wood.

"Come on." She grabbed his hand and brought him to one of the largest tables in the room filled with craft supplies. "Hey, Laura, I want you to meet my friend, Mase. He's going to help you here." Hope smirked. "Or, more like, you're going to help him."

He felt his cheeks burn bright as the young girl giggled. Mase had never met her before, but he knew she was Chief Duncan's daughter. She had long blonde hair like her mother, Lynn, and wore an elf hat like Hope. It looked like all the ladies were leaning toward elves, while the men wore Santa hats. He had yet to see anyone wearing the snowman costume. A few kids opted to be a reindeer.

"Got it. Nice to meet you, Mase."

Hope left him standing there after brushing her hand with his, but no kiss. They were in a church—and in a large room full of kids. He wouldn't complain too much. Although, he'd be getting his kiss later before he left.

"Don't worry, it's not that hard. I saw the manger you built. It's amazing. If you can do that, you can glue a pom-pom onto an ornament."

He laughed with Laura and conceded that he could figure this out. He might look a bit clumsy doing it as he had large hands and most of the things on the table were tiny. Laura introduced him to a set of twins working on snowflake ornaments. She left him alone while she helped another pair of kids.

The morning went by with fun and laughter. He learned Laura was twelve years old, in seventh grade at the local junior high school, and loved to play the violin. She liked to bake with her mom, but she loved music more, even creating some songs of her own. Just like her mother, she was full of creativity and kindness galore. Laura was wonderful with the younger kids, helping with a smile and giggles here and there. Her patience was amazing, especially with a four-year-old who kept screaming at the top of her lungs—for no particular reason. Mase watched the little girl, looking for a sign of why she was upset and a way to help, but it seemed she simply loved to scream. Her mother constantly had to tell her to quiet down and shush. Laura, being the smart one at the table, apparently, turned her screaming into singing. Suddenly, their whole table was singing about holly jolly St. Nicholas and Santa coming to town and other Christmas songs that had a peppy tune and kept the little girl engaged.

Kids cycled through, making crafts, singing, and having a great time. He didn't drop too many things. A few googly eyes might've flopped to the floor and skidded under the table. Whoops. Damn big hands.

When lunchtime rolled around, the crowd started to thin and dwindle to nothing. Gregory, Laura's grandfather, and his girlfriend, Gabby, stuck around along with a few other people to help clean up. With everyone pitching in, they had the tables and chairs put away, the floor swept, and the food cleaned up.

"Thank you so much for inviting us. I had so much fun," Mia said.

Jaxson had his arm wrapped around her. "Yeah, it wasn't bad at all. It's always nice to try something different. I even made Gabby an ornament."

Mase chuckled at the angel ornament Jaxson had decorated for his partner and best friend. It was painted white with googly eyes, making it look more comical than angelic. Gabby would love it.

"Well, later this afternoon, the firehouse is putting on a snowman building contest to raise money. All proceeds will go to the local shelter. They need more supplies. Clothes, food, toiletries, and whatnot. It's a fifty-dollar entry and the winner gets a basket filled with goodies from the local businesses around town. Lynn donated a fifty-dollar gift card to Sweet Treat Delights. It's worth it for that, in my opinion." Hope's eyes lit up at the prospect of winning.

"Did you enter?" Mase asked. He'd be more than happy to build a snowman with her.

Hell, he'd be happy doing anything with her. He enjoyed spending time with Hope.

"No, but you should." She smiled at Mia and Jaxson as if talking more to them than him. Which was odd.

"I'm game," Jaxson said with a lot more enthusiasm than he had for the crafts activity.

"I'll sign up, too." He waited for Hope to look at him. "You can be my partner."

In more ways than just snowman building.

"I'll still be at work."

"It's for a good cause. I'm sure you can dip out a little early for a good cause."

Her eyes twinkled with mischief. "I'll talk to Father Benson and see what I can do."

This time he wasn't going to let her pull away. He stepped closer, wrapped an arm around her, and kissed her senseless. He heard his brother chuckle but didn't stop to glare at him or tell him to knock it off. Feeling her lips and hearing her low whimper of approval was all he wanted to focus on.

"Be there or be square."

Her sweet laughter filled the room and his heart as she shook her head and rolled her eyes. "You're ridiculous."

"And you love it." He winked.

She jerked.

He paused, wondering at her reaction. Hmm...

Maybe she loved more than just his humor.

He could only hope.

"Now you do your best to win. I wouldn't mind if you brought some goodies to work with you from Sweet Treat Delights."

Hope chuckled along with Father Benson and the teasing laughter in his tone.

"I'll try my best for you. Thanks for letting me dip out of work early to join the fun."

"Of course. Anytime, Hope, dear. You do so much around here. You have no idea how much you make my life easier."

His eyes didn't lie. She could see the gratitude written in his gaze. It was nice to know she wasn't failing at everything. Because every other aspect of her life seemed like nothing but chaos.

This morning had been fun with Mase, despite not being around him much. She had floated around the room helping wherever she had been needed. Grabbing more supplies. Refilling the refreshment table. Making sure everyone had a smile on their face and the room was full of merriment.

While she enjoyed spending time with Mase, there were times he made her nervous. Like he wanted more out of their relationship than what she was willing to give. Sure, meeting his brother hadn't been as terrible as she thought, but still. Ugh. She couldn't even interpret her own feelings; how in the world would she try to explain anything to Mase?

And you love it.

Yeah, she wouldn't deny she loved his humor. It was refreshing to be with a guy who could make her laugh at the drop of a hat. Even when she didn't want to laugh.

Yet, when he said that, all she heard was one word— love.

It was too soon for that intense emotion. Hearing it was too much. No matter how many times she ran different scenarios in her head, she couldn't figure out how to distance herself from him.

Because she didn't want to. Because, damn it....she did kind of love him.

It was the chaotic part inside her that felt like she had to keep her distance. To deny that love was really there. She didn't like the internal emotional war raging inside her. She didn't know how to control it. How to steer or navigate it.

"You okay, Hope?"

She jerked, realizing she had zoned out on Father Benson. "Oh, of course. I'm trying to mentally prepare how I'm going to decorate my snowman."

Or snowwoman. Maybe she'd give her creation some boobs. That would be fun. Not that she'd say something like that to Father Benson. She pressed her lips together to keep from laughing. Sometimes her thoughts were too outrageous, especially for a priest.

"I'm sure it'll be amazing. Like you."

Time to go. She could only handle so many compliments before she'd go insane.

"You have a wonderful night, Father Benson."

He wished her well and ventured off down the hallway. She headed the opposite way and rushed to her car as soon as she stepped outside. It was cold as shit out.

Maybe she should've bowed out of this activity because she wasn't looking forward to freezing her ass off.

Well, at least Mase would be with her. He could warm her up.

There she went again with her wishy-washy feelings. One minute wanting to keep her distance from him, and the next, needing to be as close as possible to him.

Parking near city hall was full, so she drove down Main Street and parked close to the diner. She wound her scarf tighter around her neck, shoving her plain white knit hat farther down her head. No fun holiday props for her head right now. Being warm was her mission until this was over.

She waved hi, offering greetings as she strolled past people. The contest was being held in the park in front of city hall by the gazebo. They had a huge dumping of snow at the beginning of the month, but they did bring in a truckload for the event so everyone had enough to make their snowman.

She saw Mase standing near the signup table next to Jaxson and Mia and a man she didn't know.

"Hey, you made it." Mase leaned in for a kiss, and she nearly sighed in contentment at his hot lips warming her up.

"I still need to sign up." She looked toward the table where they were taking registration, noting it wasn't too busy. Most people had already entered. It was supposed to start in ten minutes.

"Already done. I signed us up as partners."

She shivered. That word again.

He frowned, yet didn't say anything.

What, she couldn't shiver from the cold? Because it was cold out. She wasn't about to admit she might've also shivered from the word partners.

"Awesome. I can't wait." She rubbed her hands together with glee, hoping to dispel the sudden awkward tension.

"I want you to meet my best friend and partner in crime, Cam," Mase said, slapping the guy she didn't recognize on the back with a jovial smile. "I can't believe you guys haven't met yet. It's about time. Cam, my man, this is my beautiful girlfriend, Hope."

This time she froze, her insides jittering with unease.

Girlfriend?

That word was worse than partners.

She snapped out of her shock and thrust her hand out when Cam held his out.

"It's nice to finally meet you. I swear this joker was making you up."

She laughed with everyone at Cam's comment, yet she didn't find anything funny.

Girlfriend.

Ugh. Was she ready for such a big label? She didn't think so. Or was she?

It was too much! She didn't know what the hell she wanted.

The conversation shifted—thankfully—and she stood quietly trying to snap herself out of a sour mood she could sense coming. Mase wrapped an arm around her shoulder and pulled her into his embrace. She didn't fight him. One, because she didn't want to explain why she would do such a thing. Two, it was much warmer being in his arms than standing around on her own.

Fire Chief Nicholas Downing raised a triangle and jangled it with a metal stick.

"Attention, folks. Everyone quiet down, please."

Mase pulled her closer into his embrace, and she couldn't help but rest her head against him. Silence fell around the park. It felt good to be next to him, and not because of the cold. When his arms were around her, everything made sense in her messed-up world.

"Welcome! So glad to see so many people here today. This is the first time we're having this event to help raise money for the shelter. It seriously warms my heart to see so many people here. And as cold as it is outside, I need anything to help warm me up."

Everyone chuckled with the fire chief. Hope nearly rolled her eyes at his lame joke but resisted. Because he was right. Seeing so many people show up for this was great. Nothing like a small town banding together to help others out.

"So, the rules are simple. You'll have thirty minutes to build a snowman using whatever is in the park. We do have areas filled with sticks, bark, rocks, carrots, hats, you name it. If you happen to see anything else lying around the ground, it's fair game. No pulling anything out of your bags, though. Only what's visible. Fair enough. There will be three judges. Myself, Chief Duncan, and of course, our wonderful mayor, Mayor Hafferty. Any questions before we begin?"

As soon as Hope heard the mayor would be one of the

judges, she rolled her eyes. It didn't matter how amazing she made her snowman, the mayor would never vote for hers. Whatever. That man could suck it.

"You okay?" Mase whispered, kissing the side of her head.

"I'm fine."

The last thing she wanted to do was get into why she hated the mayor and why they wouldn't be winning.

Only a few people had some questions, like how would the creations be judged? Each judge would give a score out of one through ten, and the person—or group—with the most points would win. Points would be awarded for creativity, style, and how much fun you were having. Hope knew right then she wouldn't get a great score on fun because she couldn't even smile. What a silly thing to add to being judged. Having fun? Geesh. It was the dumbest thing she ever heard.

"Okay, let's do this, people. I'll ring my gong," the fire chief said, holding up his triangle, "to announce it's started. As soon as you hear it again, that means time is up. You'll put your snow down and back away slowly from your snowman."

More laughter rang throughout the crowd. Hope only snorted at his lameness once again.

"Good luck, and most of all, have fun!"

The gong rang with merry.

Jaxson and Mia ran with laughter to the spot they had picked out, as did Cam, who was building one on his own. Mase grabbed her hand with a gentle smile and guided her to the spot he had picked for them. About thirty groups—some together, some building on their own—were sprinkled around the park ready to win.

"I'll start the bottom. You want to start the middle ball?"

She nodded at Mase, still devoid of a smile, and started rolling her ball together.

"Gosh, some people are really quick. They already have two balls done."

She barely glanced at where Mase pointed to a couple on the other side of the park. Apparently, some people were taking this way too seriously. Sure, a basket full of goodies would be nice to win, but it wasn't that big of a deal.

Why even bother? The mayor hated her. The entire time she worked for him, he had never treated her with much respect. Expected her to do everything under the sun without so much as a thank you. Working long hours. Rarely had weekends off. People thought he was a great guy, friendly, cared about the town, when in reality, he was a self-centered, egotistical jerk. Quitting—after he rudely dissed her sister—was the best thing she ever did.

She would never win this because he would never give her a decent vote.

She shrieked and shivered as a handful of snow hit her face, some slithering down the inside collar of her jacket. She looked over at Mase, who wore a devious grin and held another snowball in his hand.

"I need you to give me a smile or I will throw this one, too."

"Are you serious right now?" She tilted her head, eyeing the snow in his hand and the determination in his gaze.

"Am I?"

Her eyes narrowed.

His hand went higher.

She stuck her tongue out.

The ball went flying in the air and hit her in the chest.

"Oh, game on."

She scooped up her own snowball and threw it his way.

He dodged the blow, creating another ball, and threw it her way. They went back and forth until she couldn't hold back any longer. Laughter fell out.

Mase lunged at her, grabbing a handful of snow, and shoved it in her face. She squealed at the brutal coldness and snatched another handful, shoving it in his jacket near his neck. He shivered, yet didn't get off her.

"You will pay for this," she whispered with a devious glint in her eyes and—because she couldn't stop it—a small smile.

"I'm okay with any punishment you give me. I just wanted to see a smile on your face. I wish you'd tell me what's going on. For some reason, I think it's because I called you my girlfriend."

Well, yeah, that had bugged her, but it wasn't the reason for her surliness right now.

"I hate the mayor. He'll never give us a good score because he doesn't like me either. He hates my sister and the fact she's engaged to Stu."

Mase frowned. Either from what she said or because she ignored the thing about being his girlfriend.

"Who cares?"

"That he hates me and my sister? I care."

"No, what he thinks of you. That's his problem that he doesn't see how amazing and wonderful you are. Not yours. Don't let him take the fun out of this. Don't let him diminish your beautiful smiles. I need them. They make me happy."

Oh, why did he have to go and get all mushy and say such sweet things? She couldn't stand it. Compliments always gave her the jitters, especially from a guy. Normally, the compliments were a way to get in her pants and screw her over in more ways than one.

But not Mase. Never him. He said sweet things because he meant them—and with no ulterior motive in mind.

"Yo, bro, get a room. You two are gonna lose being all lovey-dovey over there."

Hope turned her head slightly at Jaxson, who shook his head, laughing.

Mase didn't look at his brother, his sole focus on her. His eyes searing into her as if, if he stared hard enough, he'd be able to see everything she hid from the world.

"I want a snowman as tall as you. With a goofy-ass grin to match yours."

Mase laughed. "Wow. I have a goofy-ass grin? I guess I'll take it. Let's do this."

"First, give me a kiss. To apologize for hitting me with a snowball."

He cocked a brow. "You deserved that. But I'll give you a kiss for the hell of it."

His lips met hers, warming her up for a brief moment until his lips drifted away. He helped her up and smacked her ass, which was sort of awkward with him wearing gloves and the large winter coat she had on.

They resumed rolling their balls. This time she made sure to keep a smile on her face, especially when she would glance at him and he made a gesture as if he'd throw another snowball her way.

Her irritation from before withered away. She had fun with Mase creating what she thought was the most epic snowman ever. As she requested, the snowman was nearly as tall as Mase, and he was super tall, almost six feet. They grabbed bark for the eyes and buttons for its body, placing five buttons total. A large carrot darted out for a nose, and sticks were used to curve into the cheesiest-ass grin she had ever seen on a snowman. They grabbed two sticks with evergreen leaves on the end for arms and formed an evergreen crown in place of a hat.

They stepped back to admire their creation as the gong rang throughout the park.

"Just in the nick of time," Mase said. Then he turned toward her and kissed her. "It doesn't matter if we win or not. I had fun with you."

She had so much fun as well.

But she wanted to win.

Mase chuckled and wound an arm around her shoulder as if he knew exactly what she was thinking.

"Should we name him?"

Her lips curled into a grin. "Will he come alive and be our friend if we do?"

"If he does, are you going to go dancing in the street with him?"

Hope eyed the snowman. She knew it would never come alive, but she was always game for something ridiculous.

"I'll be the first one in line, singing and dancing."

Mase squeezed her. "Let's name him Domino."

She busted out laughing. "Odd, but I like it."

"Well, it got you to laugh, so that's all that I care about."

Then Fire Chief Downing was ringing the gong again, asking for everyone's attention.

Hope looked at Domino, smiling, wishing inside they would win. She swore for one brief moment, Domino had smiled in return with a wink, telling her she had already won.

6

MASE BLEW out a breath as the judges walked away from their snowman. Then he looked at Hope, who he swore was giving the mayor such an evil glare, she would melt him in his spot.

"It's not a bad score."

She huffed. "We only got twenty-two out of thirty. Not nearly enough to win. He purposely only gave us six points. Six!"

Mase was smart enough to hold in his laughter, even though he could feel it bubbling up inside. She was adorable when she got mad over something so silly. It was just a contest. The important part about the entire event was the money raised for the shelter. But he also knew she had bad blood with the mayor, so she was taking it personally.

"Well, we got two scores of eight from the other two. That's not bad."

She turned toward him, frowning. "It's my fault. I didn't have enough fun. We got screwed on the fun score part."

He leaned in and kissed her neck. "You can make it up to me later. Show me what kind of fun is hiding in there."

She giggled when he nuzzled her neck again.

Jaxson and Mia joined them, as did Cam, as soon as their snow creations were scored. They all received a twenty-four, getting eight points for each category. They chatted while the judges scored the rest around the park. They decided they'd venture to the diner for a bite to eat and something warm to drink to heat them up from the cold that was starting to numb them to the bone.

Mase pulled Hope closer into his side when the fire chief rang the gong again to announce the winner. The crowd cheered for Serenity and her twin boys, Royce and Randall, when they won with the only score of thirty. They had created not one snowman, but three of them, making a wonderful family of snow people. They had even created a small snow house. Mase was impressed they even managed to create so much in so little time. Thirty minutes wasn't a lot of time to do much.

Hope laughed.

Mase followed her gaze, where she watched Laura walk with Chief Duncan to congratulate the family. Mase knew right away why Hope laughed. Because the boys, who looked to be about Laura's age, were handsome fellows, and even from the distance they stood, he could see Laura's bright-red cheeks. He didn't think that was from the cold.

"Oh, to be young again."

He chuckled and kissed her cheek. "Ready to head to the diner?"

"I've been ready." She shivered as if she meant to, but he didn't think so. The wind was starting to pick up speed and slap them in the faces a little too much.

With them in the lead, Cam trailing with Jaxson and Mia behind him, they headed for the diner. It was packed. Everyone had the same idea as they did.

They managed to snag the circular booth near the opposite end from the door where they would all fit without breathing on each other.

"I only want a slice of pie and a hot chocolate. I'll be right back."

Hope dashed toward the bathroom before he could ask what kind of pie. Cam scooted in next to him. Jaxson sat on his other side with, of course, Mia on his other side.

Jaxson leaned in. "Everything cool with Hope?"

"Yeah. She needed to use the bathroom."

"She did act a little weird for a moment there," Cam added as if Jaxson hadn't been talking about her walking away just now.

Jaxson nodded as if he knew what Cam was referring to. Mase had no clue what either was talking about.

"When?"

Mia chuckled and stood up. "I need to use the bathroom, too. I'll have whatever you're having." She kissed Jaxson and walked away.

"Great. Look what you did." Mase swung a hand toward Mia. "Who knows what she's about to say to Hope."

Jaxson's brows rose. "Mia's the last person to get into anyone's business, unless it's Gabby. She needs to use the bathroom. Not to mention, give us time to chat so you can tell us what's up with Hope."

"Yep. Gotta tell us. If you can't tell your best friend and your brother, then something's wrong."

Mase shrugged. "No clue what I'm supposed to tell you. Hope is fine." And Mase wasn't about to add to Cam that he didn't always share his every woe with him. He was one to talk.

Of course, when he had asked back in the park if she

was okay and she had answered with she was fine, he hadn't believed her. Hence the throwing of the snowball to get her out of whatever mood she had been in.

"It...she seemed off." Jaxson mirrored his shrug.

"Kind of started when you mentioned the word girlfriend," Cam added.

Oh, that.

Yeah, he had noticed the same weird reaction from her. She had covered it up quickly, but not enough where he had missed it.

He grabbed a menu from the middle of the table and opened it.

This was not something he wanted to talk about, especially in such a crowded place where anyone could hear.

"You seriously have nothing for us?" Jaxson asked.

He shrugged again. "I don't know what to say. I noticed it. I haven't exactly had a chance to talk to her about it. Maybe I'm moving too fast with her."

Jaxson clapped him on the shoulder. "You know how I feel. I was leery about her from the get-go when you told me about her. I don't want you to get hurt. Be careful."

Yeah, Mase knew how Jaxson felt about her. It had caused some tension between them in the beginning. Thankfully, Jaxson had lessened his irritation about Hope and hadn't once—since he arrived in town—made her feel unwelcome. He appreciated his brother's support, even though he was iffy about her.

"I will. Now knock it off."

Jaxson gave him a devilish grin as if he would table the conversation—for now. Then he looked around the diner. "There's only one person working behind the counter. We could be waiting a while for some service."

Mase saw Theresa bouncing from table to table with an extra pep in her step. The diner obviously hadn't anticipated people from the event flocking there afterward, especially since it was the first time the event had taken place. Well, if they did it next year, they'd know to be more prepared.

"We have no plans for the night, so I guess not a big deal." At least, it wasn't to Mase.

"Yeah, I'm cool," Cam said, relaxing, propping an arm across the back of the booth.

Chief Duncan walked into the diner with Lynn, Laura, and their youngest daughter, Eloise, in tow. Mase smiled when Lynn chatted with Theresa and then headed behind the counter. He saw another woman he didn't recognize also head behind the counter to help. Chief Duncan and his kids had taken a seat with Bentley, a local firefighter he had met once. Mase could only assume that was his wife or girlfriend who had decided to help as well. A little boy who looked close to two years old sat next to Bentley. He and Eloise, who he knew was almost three, immediately started chatting in the cute way toddlers did.

The ladies came back to the table before anyone had approached the booth yet. Cam slid out for Hope to slide in and then resumed his seat.

"Wow, this place is hopping," Mia commented. "No one came by yet?"

"Nope. It might be a while. But I saw two people step in to help." One nice thing about living in a small town, Mase thought. People helping people.

"You know, I'll see if Theresa needs my help, too." Hope smiled, then looked at Cam to move.

Cam looked at him first, for some strange reason, as if asking for permission to move, but when he didn't respond in any way, Cam slid out. It wasn't his call whether Hope helped or not. He didn't have any say over her. Hope whisked away toward Theresa, chatting a moment before dipping behind the counter as well.

"I like small towns. This is so nice," Mia commented. "And I don't mind we have to wait a bit. It's going to take forever to warm up my hands."

"No joke," Cam said with a laugh.

Jaxson grabbed Mia's hands and started to rub them together with his.

The gesture was sweet and endearing. It made him wonder if Hope would mind if he did something like that— in public. Sure, behind closed doors he didn't think she'd care. They had been somewhat adventurous in their sexual endeavors. He liked how open she was about her sexuality, up for trying anything. But she seemed to shy away more often than not when they were in public, where anyone could see them.

It hurt. Only because he loved her.

He was worried he'd never receive the sentiment in return.

"You are all such saviors. You have no idea." Theresa blew out a breath before grabbing another plate from Bonzo.

Lynn was shuffling behind the counter pouring coffee and making hot chocolates. Emma bustled from table to table taking orders and delivering them, along with Hope.

"Girl, I don't think anyone expected everyone to flock here." Hope chuckled. "But I'm sure Bonzo isn't complaining. He loves big crowds."

"Yeah, well, we know for next time." Theresa chuckled along with her.

"Honestly, you should take a seat. We can handle this," Emma said as her eyes honed in on Theresa's big belly. She grabbed another plate Bonzo just set out on the windowsill.

"Please," Theresa said, rolling her eyes, "I can handle this. And I'll make Aiden give me the best massage in the world tonight because I know my feet will be killing me."

Then, before any of them could argue with her, she jaunted away with two plates in her hands.

Hope knew Theresa could be stubborn. She'd keel over before she stopped and took a break, even five months pregnant.

"It's useless to argue with her," Lynn said, then set a hot steaming cup of coffee in front of Bernie. "If Aiden wasn't working, he'd make her sit down while he did her work, but he's about the only one who'd probably get her to relax."

Hope agreed, so it was pointless to argue with Theresa. Best just to get to work and stop fretting about it.

She grabbed one of the hot chocolates Lynn had prepared and headed for the table where Mase and the gang sat. She set the hot chocolate in front of Mia.

"I know you wanted one. What can I get everyone else?"

They hadn't talked much in the bathroom. She had mentioned she was dying for a hot chocolate, and Mia had reciprocated the same thing. Mia mentioned how much fun she had as well and thanked her for inviting her to the event, but otherwise, not much was said. Which Hope was okay with. She didn't need someone she barely knew trying to get in her head and talk about her shit.

Mase's mouth curved into a sultry grin. "Surprise me, sweetheart."

She trembled at the endearment but didn't falter in the

gentle smile on her face. She would not let it show how much his silly—oh so sweet—endearment sounded coming from his smooth lips. He also had no idea how much it meant to her when Cam looked at him for approval to move like she needed some sort of permission to help her friends out and he had ignored him. Oh, hell, no. No man was going to boss her around. But Mase didn't say or do a thing. He simply waited for Cam to get the hell out of her way. He would never know how much that meant to her. And now calling her such a wonderful pet name.

He should be careful with what he said. Who knew what she might surprise him with?

"Okay, one mincemeat pie coming right up." She pretended to jot it down on her imaginary notepad.

She had a decent memory. In her teenage years, she had worked at the diner, so this wasn't anything new for her. During the summer, Bonzo was great about hiring a few local teens to help them earn a bit of cash before they ventured off to college.

Mase winced and frowned.

Hope only laughed. Because she knew he hated mincemeat pie.

"Oh, I love that kind. I'll take one, too," Jaxson piped in.

Hope's eyes bulged. "Seriously? I hate that pie, too."

"I love it." Jaxson's laughter filled the entire area. "Oh, man, you should've seen Mase every Christmas when our gram was alive. He always ate a piece for her, and the torture on his face as he did was always so hilarious. She always thought you loved that pie, too."

"The things I do for love." Mase shrugged, then looked her dead in the eye.

She shivered again, this time from his piercing look, as if he were telling her *give me the pie, I'll eat it because I love you.*

No, she wasn't ready for that emotion, even if sometimes she felt it deep in her soul.

"I'll take a piece of apple pie, and thank you for the hot chocolate. It's delicious." Mia picked up the mug to take another sip, bliss glittering in her eyes.

"I'll take a coffee and no pie," Cam said, then tapped the menu. "The roast beef sounds delicious."

"You know, the club sandwich sounded good. You want to split one?" Jaxson asked Mia.

Mia nodded. "That does sound good."

"Okay. I'll be right back soon with everything. Bonzo is the best in the kitchen."

Hope walked away, deciding the club sandwich sounded good to her as well. She'd split one with Mase, considering he said to surprise him. The fries it came with were the best. The seasoning Bonzo used—which he refused to share— was off the charts. So damn delicious.

She put in the orders and grabbed Mia's slice of pie, dropping it off at the table before dashing off to help more customers.

The night flew by with laughter and merriment. Everyone understood that things were moving slower than normal because of the heavy presence. Her feet were killing her by the time she sat down next to Mase. Cam had graciously—once again—moved for her to slide in. Two portions of the club sandwich were still on the plate with a small pile of fries. She could've kissed him thoroughly for saving her some of the fries without her even asking him to.

"You're amazing, Hope. That was so nice of you to help out," Mia said as she took a sip of her hot chocolate, which looked to be almost gone.

"That's what we do around here. Help out when needed. Theresa would do the same for any of us."

Hope took a huge chunk out of the sandwich and sighed with pleasure as the delicious flavors swirled around her mouth. Gosh, one of these days she'd pry the secret sauce Bonzo added to the sandwich out of him. Somehow, someway.

"Hey, so did Mase mention Christmas Eve yet?" Jaxson asked as casually as if he were talking about some new show that everyone was binging lately.

Hope forced herself to keep smiling when she wanted to frown like the saddest clown on earth.

"No, he hasn't."

Mase cleared his throat and looked at Jaxson funny before looking at her. "I know you're spending Christmas Day with your family, but if you don't have plans for Christmas Eve, we'd love for you to join us. Afternoonish. We're having a turkey for supper."

Oh, shit. How could she possibly say no, in front of everyone?

Mase had known the last time she lied and it had been via text. He'd definitely know it with her sitting right next to him.

"Yeah, sure. I don't have plans. I mean, I'm visiting my grandpa, but I can visit him in the morning instead of the afternoon."

"If you don't mind switching your plans?"

"Not at all." Although the chaotic nerves swirling in her stomach said a completely different story.

Mase kissed her. "Great. Cam's coming, too."

"Fifth wheel. Yay me," Cam cheered sarcastically, yet the smile on his face said he didn't mind.

"I saw you eyeing Serenity when they were announcing the winners." Mase chuckled. "I heard she's single."

Hope frowned. Where in the world did he hear that and why did he care?

"With twin boys," Cam added as his eyes went round. "You don't ask a single mother over for Christmas Eve, especially when I've never even spoken to her."

"Yeah, I agree with Cam on that one," Jaxson said with a chuckle as he shook his head.

"Well, for the future, now you know she's single. Maybe not Christmas Eve, but you should ask her out."

It rankled her nerves once again when he said it.

She was not a jealous woman.

Well, on occasion she could be, but considering she didn't do *serious* serious relationships often, jealousy usually didn't come into play.

"Should I bring something? I can swing by and grab something from Lynn's bakery." Hope chuckled. "Because, let's be honest, I am not a baker."

Mase squeezed her into his side and kissed her cheek. "Just your beautiful self. You're in luck. Jaxson is the ultimate baker and will be busy in the kitchen."

"Those salted nut rolls are already calling my name," Jaxson said as he rubbed his belly.

Hope had no idea what kind of treat salted nut rolls were, but they sounded delicious.

"Ok, I'll bring myself."

Oh, crap. And presents for everyone. She couldn't show up on Christmas Eve without bringing a little something for Mia, Jaxson, and Cam. Of course, she had bought Mase something. Nothing extravagant.

Because they were...having some fun. Some great sex.

But since he had muttered the word girlfriend, she might have to up her gift for him as well.

She shivered. Girlfriend. She still wasn't sure what to think of that.

"You okay?" Mase whispered in her ear.

She turned his way and offered a smile, despite the turmoil coursing through her veins. "Never better."

The way his eyes slightly narrowed, she knew he sensed her lying once again.

7

"Yeah, okay, I got it. I'll do it." Hope slammed her car door a little harder than she intended.

"If you don't want to, you don't have to. I just thought it'd be a nice thing, especially since he invited you over today."

Hope barely withheld a heavy sigh. She knew Chasity was only trying to cheer her up and make her see things differently. Inviting Mase and his family over for Christmas Day shouldn't be a big deal. But it was. She was still trying to come to terms with the fact she was going over to his house for Christmas Eve. The holidays should be a happy, merry time, and since she woke up this morning she had been dragging her feet to even get out the door.

She couldn't disappoint Father Preston and miss Christmas Eve mass. He expected her at Christmas mass as well. Not that she had plans to miss Christmas mass. But even getting ready for church had been a trial, making her feel guilty the entire time that she was dreading going. Once she got to church and settled in the pew, a bit of her turmoil had settled. She had even said a silent prayer that the day would go well. As soon as she walked out—after taking care of a few things in her office—the disorder causing havoc in her body went into full force once again.

Why the hell wasn't her sister mad when she told her the change of plans? She was supposed to be spending Christmas Eve with her, Stu, and Grandpa in the afternoon. Chasity barely batted an eye, sounding way too cheery when she told her the change of plans yesterday. It had taken her over a day to even tell her sister about it. So pathetic.

"It's cool. I'll invite them. No big deal."

"If it wasn't a big deal, it'd sound like it. If you're not serious about Mase, you need to tell him."

This time Hope did let out an exasperated sigh. Why did her sister have to do this to her now? Why couldn't she have brought up all of this when she told her the change of plans? Ridiculous.

"My blow dryer broke this morning, I'm irritated about that. Okay. I like Mase, and I don't mind whatsoever inviting him to Christmas."

Lies!

Although, she had to give herself props because the lie came out pretty smooth. Except the part about her blow-dryer. It stopped working for her halfway through drying her hair. That had been her first sign it was going to be the worst Christmas Eve ever. She couldn't dry her hair, and if she didn't, it dried in a weird wavy mess, and she wanted to look good for Mase. Instead, she had to throw her hair into a ponytail. She added a red scrunchie with a large white pom-pom on it for a bit of Christmas cheer. Too bad it didn't elevate her mood.

Chasity returned a sigh, knowing full well Hope wasn't being completely honest. "Great. Say hi to Grandpa for me. I'll be there later this afternoon."

Duh! Of course, she didn't utter that sarcastic word because she didn't want to hurt her sister. They both didn't need to feel like the world was coming to end. Only she needed to feel like that.

"Will do."

Hope hung up before Chasity could delve deeper into anything else. She wasn't in the mood.

For anything.

Well, except seeing her grandpa, who usually could cheer her up without an issue.

She waved hello to Nancy, who ran the front desk at the retirement home, and headed for the commons area. Her grandpa and Chuck, his best buddy in the place, sat at a small square table playing cards. She kissed him on the cheek, adding one to Chuck's cheek as well before plopping down in a chair.

"What's got my pumpkin in a mood?" The concern in his eyes overshadowed the smile on his lips. Her grandpa had always been a very astute man, picking up on the littlest things. She didn't even get out the word hello and he was sensing her turbulent mood.

He had been her rock since she could remember, all the way from when she was a little girl. Chasity, too. They were both close to their grandpa. While he called Chasity Pumpernickel, he liked to call her Pumpkin. Which was ironic—and probably the reason he did—because she didn't like pumpkin anything. No pumpkin spice latte, no pumpkin pie, nothing whatsoever pumpkin. Gross!

"I'm fine. Merry Christmas Eve. What are we playing?" She inched up her smile a notch, hoping to disguise the turmoil beneath her facade.

Chuck stopped brushing the cards his way and cocked a brow. "Even I can tell that's a bunch of hocus-pocus."

Hope giggled, despite her crabby mood. "It's Christmas, not Halloween. I'm fine." Her smile fell a fraction. "Mostly fine."

"Where's this young man of yours I keep hearing about? Is that what has my pumpkin in a gloomy mood?"

"He's with his family. His brother and his fiancée are visiting for the holidays. I'll be joining them later." She sighed as she took the cards Chuck pushed her way and cut the deck before pushing it back toward him. "I don't know. It feels like it's moving so fast. And let's face it, Grandpa, I have terrible judgment in men. They all suck."

Her grandpa and Chuck laughed, nodding their heads. "I hear nothing but good things about him. What does that gut of yours say? You can always trust your gut. Problem is, you ignore it sometimes, and you know it."

His stern expression said he knew her all too well. She wouldn't dispute anything he said. It was true. Her gut had told her Tyrone was no good. That he had a possessive streak that wasn't healthy. What did she do anyway? Dated him until he caused damage around town, getting into a fight with Mase like he had a right to fight for her or something. If she had stayed any longer, that possessive streak would've turned potentially deadly. Him grabbing her arm so roughly had said he would've turned violent sooner or later. No, thanks. She deserved better than that.

Bottom line, she attracted dead-beat assholes, losers, and the bad-boy types.

Except maybe Mase. He did seem to be one of the good ones. And for some scary, odd reason, it frightened the hell out of her. How did she deal with a good guy? What happened if she said the wrong thing, did the wrong thing? In the end, she was likely to screw it all up. So why even bother?

"Hope." The way her grandpa said her name told her she wouldn't be escaping any of his questions. Not quite a demand, but it wasn't said questioningly.

"He's amazing. He's one of the good ones, and I'm bound to screw it up."

Her grandpa laid a hand over hers. "You can't screw up a good thing. Not something that's meant to be. If it's meant to be, it is. Stop worrying so much about things and have fun. Embrace what's developing between you two." His eyes narrowed. "And bring the fellow here so I can make my own judgment."

"Yep. Me, too," Chuck added as if he were her honorary grandpa or something. Which he sort of was. Whenever she visited her grandpa, Chuck was always there.

That was a good idea—and terrifying all in one. If her grandpa hated Mase, which she highly doubted would ever happen, she knew the relationship would never work.

Come to think of it, the few guys her grandpa had met, he despised each one.

Maybe that was another reason she was scared to bring Mase to meet her grandpa. If he didn't like Mase, she knew everything would fall apart sooner rather than later.

"I'll bring him soon. I promise."

"I'm holding you to that, pumpkin." Her grandpa turned to Chuck. "Now deal the cards. Afterward, we'll go snag some of those butter horns I see." He leaned closer to her. "Make sure to grab at least two. So good."

Hope giggled. Oh, yeah, he wanted her to grab two. One for her, and one for him. While he grabbed his own. The sneaky guy.

They played cards, laughing, having fun. A few of the other residents stopped by to wish her Merry Christmas. The place, as usual, was decked in holiday delight. Wreaths on the doors to the room. A Christmas tree in the corner. A few paintings with holiday scenes hanging on the walls. The place, along with her grandpa and Chuck, helped to raise her spirits.

By the time she left, heading back home, she wasn't dreading going to Mase's as much. She changed, grabbed the presents, and dashed to her car. On the drive to his house, her nerves started to attack her once again.

It won't be bad. All will go well.

She kept repeating that mantra in her head over and over until she believed it—partially. She couldn't help herself. Half the time, she lived like a glass-half-empty kind of girl. The other half, she tried to live like a glass-half-full. It was a hard balancing act.

Silence permeated the air as she cut the car off. Mase's house loomed before her. The lights were all on, and it looked warm and inviting. Funny, she had never been inside his house yet. Whenever she had come over, he was always in his workshop, so that's where she headed. He never asked her to spend the night—thankfully. She wasn't ready for that sort of thing. That would solidify the whole girl-friend/boyfriend thing he insisted they were.

Despite her reservations about things, the one thing she knew was she wasn't a coward. About anything.

She grabbed her purse and the presents and jaunted toward the house before she lost all her nerves.

The door opened before she could knock.

"Merry Christmas Eve." Mase took the presents from her hands and kissed her on the lips. "You look beautiful."

She doubted that, not with her disastrous hair, but it was nice of him to say so.

"You look dashing yourself." She couldn't help but grin at his adorable Christmas sweater that had two snowmen on the front throwing snowballs at each other. It was silly and ridiculous, but he managed to make it appear charming in a way. It reminded her of the snowman contest a few days ago and the snowball fight they had. Such a wonderful memory.

She hung up her coat as Mase put the presents near the tree.

"Drink? Cam's not here yet, and Jaxson's in the kitchen with Mia making way too much good food for us."

She shouldn't have too much as she planned to drive home tonight.

The intense sparkle in his eyes increased the nerves running rampant through her veins. Did he want her to sleep over? Was that what he was trying to convey?

She'd ignore it and hope that wasn't his secret message to her. A drink just might calm her nerves some.

"I'd love one."

"Wine, beer, or eggnog?"

"Oh, eggnog sounds delicious."

Mase wrapped an arm around her and guided her toward the kitchen where Jaxson and Mia were hanging out. "Mia made it. It is pretty good."

More hellos and Merry Christmases went out as she greeted Jaxson and Mia. Mase poured her a drink in a fun Christmas mug that said 'I'm on the nice list...when I'm not being naughty.' Oh, did she feel that saying in her bones. It was almost too appropriate for her. Maybe he had purchased it with her in mind.

Jaxson bustled around the kitchen like a wizard, creating smells that had her salivating to try everything he was baking. There were cookies and Christmas treats displayed on the counter. Something with an intense smell —probably the turkey—filled the air. A nice salad topped with everything under the sun sat on the table already. A feast before her, and she wanted to dig in right this second.

The first sip of the eggnog soothed her bones. The second sip had her making eye contact with Mase. The third sip, she downed the entire thing.

His gaze was still giving her the heebie-jeebies. She couldn't determine whether they were the good or bad kind.

"Come on. I want to show you something." Mase looked at Jaxson and Mia. "We'll be right back."

Then he dragged her toward the side door, slipped on a pair of shoes, and pulled her outside without warning. She hadn't taken her shoes off yet, which she should've done right away. He had distracted her with the enticement of a drink and his smoldering gaze that was making her insides gurgle with trepidation.

He led her to his workshop where the blissful warmth heated her up from the short, brutal walk outside.

Before she could say anything, he was pulling her into his arms and his lips were devouring hers.

All her worries, all her nerves, disappeared in a blink of an eye.

All that mattered was Mase and him never letting her go.

———

MASE PULLED AWAY FROM HER, hating to, but needing to.

"What do you have to show me?"

The devilish twinkle in her eyes told him he could have his wicked way with her right here and now if he wanted. He didn't think his brother would mind at all. Not that he'd share what they might do in here.

But that's not why he brought her outside.

"I actually didn't have anything to show you."

The desire in her eyes dwindled until nothing but trepidation glimmered back. Her brows lowered, even her smile disappeared.

"Well, why did we come out here?"

She instinctively knew he didn't come out here for a quick romp against his workbench. Not that he'd mind if it happened before they went back into the house.

"I haven't had a chance to talk to you without my brother or Mia around and I just..." Oh, shit. How did he have this conversation? Where to start? Hell, why was he doing it on Christmas Eve of all days?

Well, duh. He knew why. Because the more time he spent with her, the harder he was falling for her. If they weren't on the same page about things, then it would be better to rip the band-aid off right away, so to speak, rather than wait.

"And," Hope said, waving her hand in a circular motion for him to continue.

"And I felt a weird vibe when I mentioned the word girlfriend." God, that sounded so dumb. Could he be any more ridiculous?

She took a step back.

Not a good sign.

Shit.

He should've waited. Because when she broke his heart, he'd always be reminded of this moment on Christmas Eve. What a way to ruin his holiday.

"I mean, do we have to define things so soon?"

He cocked a brow as he folded his arms. "Yeah, it would be nice. I'm not here for a friend with benefits sort of thing, Hope. So I wasn't wrong that you didn't like me calling you my girlfriend?"

"It surprised me. You said we could take this at my pace. It doesn't sound like you're doing that now."

He nearly groaned but managed to swallow it. She was right, of course. He had said he wouldn't rush her, and here he was doing exactly that. But he didn't see anything wrong at defining them as a couple.

"I won't share with other guys."

Hope rolled her eyes. "I have no plans on sleeping with anyone else. I'm offended you think I would."

"I don't think you would." The way she rolled her eyes again said she didn't believe him. Honestly, he didn't think that, but it was nice to have the confirmation they were at least on the same page. "Since we're agreed on that, what is the big deal if I call you my girlfriend? We're a couple."

"No, we're...we are..." She sighed heavily.

He loosened his stance and dropped his arms to his sides. "We're what? Because I can't do just friends with sex on the side. I care about you, Hope. I need some kind of definition here or..."

Shit, shit, shit. He did not want to lose her, but he felt like he had no choice. This wasn't something he could compromise on. He shouldn't have to.

And *care* was a loose term for him. He loved her. With all his heart and soul. Of course, he knew if he even hinted at that kind of emotion she would run out of his life so fast, she'd be nothing but a blur.

She had a look in her eyes that said she was ready to bolt at the moment.

"Or?"

Hope wasn't one to hold back. She had to poke the bear inside him.

"Or maybe this isn't going to work between us."

There. He said it. And he felt like someone had taken a dull knife and shoved it straight through his heart, then twisted it for good measure.

"You're right. This isn't going to work between us. I can't give you what you want, Mase." She shook her head, pressing her lips together as if she were holding back tears, yet her eyes looked as dry as the Sahara Desert. "I wish I could. I just...I can't do this right now. I'm sorry."

She started to rush past him, but he grabbed her arm before she could escape.

"Don't leave. I'm sorry."

That was the last thing he wanted. Damn it. He should've never had this conversation tonight. He was ten kinds of an idiot.

"It's better this way. Tell Jaxson and Mia I'm sorry."

Then she pulled her arm away, and he didn't want to hurt her any more than he already was, so he let go without fighting. She closed the door quietly behind her. He watched as she headed around to the front of the house instead of going in through the back door where they had walked out from.

"Shit!"

His arm flew across his workbench, shoving the few materials and pieces of wood he had lying on there to the ground. A wrench flew so far, it put a hole in his wall.

It was poetic, in a way.

That's how his heart felt.

A huge, gaping hole. Nothing—no spackle, no new drywall, nothing that might patch that hole in the wall—would make him whole again.

When he stepped outside, he heard the rumble of her car, yet he didn't walk toward the front of the house to see her disappear. Silence greeted him when he walked back into the kitchen.

Mia was nowhere to be seen, and his brother stood by the fridge, a concerned look on his face.

"What happened?"

Mase shrugged. "I started a conversation I should've waited on."

Jaxson grabbed two beers from the fridge and handed him one. "Like what?"

"Like what the hell we are. She doesn't like that I called her my girlfriend. She doesn't want to define what the hell we are. I'm not here just for some amazing sex. I love her."

Jaxson didn't say anything at first. They both took a large swallow before he decided to speak.

"I don't know what to say, Mase."

A lame chuckle came out. "Because nothing you'd say would be nice. I know you've never had high opinions of her."

"She seems nice. I won't say I hate her. She obviously has some issues she needs to deal with before she's ready for a relationship. Maybe give her some time."

"Yeah, maybe. Damn, man, that turkey smells delicious. When will it be ready?"

His brother narrowed his eyes at first, debating whether to continue the conversation or move it along like he wanted to. Hashing it over and over would solve nothing. Jaxson was right. Perhaps all Hope needed was time. He sprung it on her and he realized that had been a mistake. He should've let it go and rode the wave.

Until it all would've come crashing down sooner or later.

In the end, it was better this way. He knew where they stood, and he could hopefully mend his broken heart a lot faster.

If it would even be possible.

Jaxson threw a smile out, deciding it was best to put the convo to the side. "Another thirty minutes and it should be good. You wanna mash the potatoes?"

"Gosh, yeah. I love mashing."

Jaxson simply grinned at his sarcastic comeback.

Maybe it would release some of the tension creating havoc in his veins.

Despite what happened—his damn fault, too—he would not let this ruin his Christmas Eve.

HOPE WAS SO proud of herself. She managed to drive home, change into her pajamas, and pour a large glass of wine before the tears came. It was silly. She had no reason to be crying. All she had to do was say 'ok, we can be a couple.' 'I don't mind being your girlfriend.' 'Exclusive is cool with me.' But no, instead she acted like a colossal ass and walked away from the best guy to ever walk into her life.

Talk about a walking disaster. Her in a nutshell.

Hell, her friend, Clarissa, in tenth grade had called her a drama queen over something so stupid she couldn't even remember what it was about. Clarissa wasn't the only person to call her that. Of course, the term had offended her and she refused to be her friend anymore—still to this day —but Clarissa hadn't been wrong.

She *was* a drama queen.

The thing between her and Mase shouldn't be that complicated. She didn't know what the hell was wrong with her. All she knew was the thought of defining them scared the hell out of her.

Bells jingled merrily as she sat up and poured wine into her glass, having devoured the first one a little too quickly.

She giggled, despite her eyes still watering. Wearing these pajamas had been a good decision. The shorts had pictures of holly leaves with two bells in the middle. On the shirt, one large holly leaf took up most of the space with two bells also on it. Of course, the holly leaf was so large the bells happened to go right where her nipples were, and they were actual bells. So when she moved, they jingled. She had bought the outfit on a whim because it made her giggle. Every time she wore it, it also made her chuckle.

The perfect outfit to cheer her up.

Of course, the moment she sat back and silence reigned in the space, her mood dipped drastically and the tears flowed a bit harder.

"You're so dumb, Hope."

Seriously. What was the big deal if he was her boyfriend? They could still be together, hang out and have fun. Have lots and lots of great sex.

Although, it wouldn't just be the sex she'd miss. Mase was one of a kind. He made her laugh with ease. He made her feel like she was special and the most important person in his life. He made her believe that love could exist.

Not that she had ever loved before. Infatuated, yep. In extreme lust, for sure. Giddy with excitement, totally.

But love, nope.

She didn't date the kind of guys that made her want to fall in love.

Until Mase.

"Now I realize my mistake."

Her head slammed against the back of the couch and she sighed. How did she make this right? Groveling didn't even seem like enough. She walked away from him on Christmas Eve. Not any old day, but a holiday. It would take a miracle for him to forgive her.

Maybe it was for the best. She was a mess. Ever since last Christmas when she quit her job, everything seemed to go downhill. Dated the loser Tyrone. Moving in with her sister

—for the short time Chasity stayed before moving in with Stu.

She felt so lost and confused and unsure of where her life was going.

The darkness and the silence wasn't helping her mood. Wiping the tears from her eyes and cheeks, she decided she couldn't have a pity party like this. It needed a better atmosphere.

She got up and plugged in her small Christmas tree that had like five ornaments on it. But the bright colored lights made up for the lack of detail. Then she grabbed the remote and flipped through the channels before stopping on a funny Christmas movie.

There. That should help a bit.

Oh, pity food.

After scrounging through her pantry, she decided on a bag of potato chips and a bowl of chocolate chip cookie dough ice cream. She couldn't forget her bag of black licorice. Nothing would be left in that bag by tomorrow morning.

She had the biggest bowl of ice cream first. Honestly, she could've eaten straight from the container, she had scooped so much of it out. In between bites she sipped her wine. By the time the bowl was all gone, even licked clean by hers truly, she had to pour another glass of wine.

A large giggle erupted as she opened the bag of chips. The sounds were just too amusing, which told her she was getting a little too drunk, if a silly sound like that made her laugh.

On Christmas Eve.

A pity party on the way to being drunk.

Merry Christmas to her.

When the movie ended, she saw the bottle of wine was

empty. Good thing she had another in the kitchen. She grabbed the bottle, smacking it on the counter with too much gusto. More giggles escaped when it really wasn't funny. She had another glass of wine ready as the next movie started. The new bottle sat near her for easy reaching.

Christmas movie marathon here she came.

The night went by in a flash as she drank her problems away and watched movies filled with happiness and way too damn much cheer. None of it helped to lift her mood.

By eleven o'clock, her eyes were drooping and her mind was spinning.

Bedtime.

In her actual bed. No way was she sleeping on her couch.

She stood up, knocking the second wine bottle over. White liquid started pouring out steadily.

"Oh, shit on a stick."

Rushing to the kitchen, she grabbed a towel and rushed back to the living room, catching her foot on the edge of the couch. She tripped, hitting her chin hard to the ground. Her tongue got caught between her teeth and the pain that erupted made her scream.

A few explicit words might've slipped out, too.

She tasted the metallic flavor of blood as she wiped up the wine mess as best as she could. The towel got soaked immediately. Rubbing her tongue along the edge of her mouth did nothing to soothe her pain. Tears started to pool in her eyes once again. This time from actual physical pain.

Well, at least she hadn't been drinking red wine tonight. That would've nailed the rest of her coffin shut, staining her nice white carpet with red wine. She should be thankful for small favors.

A few tears slid down as she threw the wet towel in the

kitchen sink. Whatever else was left to pick up would have to be cleaned tomorrow. She'd have to get the shampoo vacuum out and clean it thoroughly as she could still smell the wine in the air as she walked back to the couch to grab her phone.

Besides hanging out with her sister—and other people she didn't even want to think about—she didn't have much on her plans tomorrow. She could have pity party number two while she finished cleaning her mess. Oh, and going to church. Maybe she could cleanse a bit of her soul while she was there.

She'd have to grab more wine from the liquor store.

Oh, shit.

Nothing would be open as it would be Christmas Day tomorrow. What a way to ruin her day.

She wobbled toward her bedroom, hitting the wall more often than she cared to admit. Everything seemed so blurry and out of focus.

She nearly fell again when she closed her bedroom door. Then, because fate was a cruel thing, she did fall, misjudging how far away her bed was situated. She landed hard on the floor.

Defeated, she lay there, staring at the ceiling in the dark. Perhaps turning on the lights would've helped her muddled state of mind.

A loud crash startled her, bolting her upright.

Crawling on her hands and knees, she rushed to her door and flipped the locked. Pressing her head against the door, she listened.

What was that noise? It had sounded like glass breaking.

Her window? Her sliding door? She was on the ground level in an apartment building. If someone was breaking in, it wouldn't be that hard.

Oh, shit on a stick.

Fumbling with her phone, it took several attempts before she could put in the passcode.

She still couldn't hear anything else, like someone moving around. That didn't mean someone hadn't broken in.

The grip she had on her phone was so strong, she swore she was bound to crush it into pieces.

What did she do?

Who did she call?

Or was she so drunk she was imagining things?

8

He reached for his phone on his nightstand, glancing at the clock at the same time.

11:05 p.m.

It was late. Who the hell was calling him so damn late, and on Christmas Eve?

His hand shook as he saw the caller.

Hope.

What did it mean? Was she calling to apologize? Was he ready for that? He wasn't sure how many more beatings he could take from her before she officially broke him beyond repair.

It rang five times before he had the nerve to answer.

"Oh, my, God, Mase. I think somens in my house."

Whoa! Okay, not what he expected. He bolted to his feet as the hair on his arms stood up, little goose bumps appearing. She sounded funny, too.

"Where are you?"

"In me house, dummy."

Slurred, messed-up words.

"Are you drunk, Hope?"

"Soooooooo. Are you not be listening to me? Somens in my house."

Right. Somens meant someone, and she sounded scared as if she wasn't making it up. Of course, he didn't know why she'd lie about something like that. Clearly, she was drunk, though. Maybe her mind was conjuring things that weren't there.

"Did you call the police? I'll be right there."

"I called you. I need you."

I need you. A stab straight to the heart. Did she mean it? Or was it her drunken-hazed mind saying it?

"I'll be right there."

He jaunted downstairs, grabbing a jacket and his keys, and was out of his house in under a minute.

"Where are you in your house?" Considering he already tried to ask that question, he figured he had to be a bit more specific about what he meant.

Silence answered him.

"Hope?"

He glanced at his phone before starting his truck. She was still on the line. Then why wasn't she answering him?

"Hope?"

Still nothing. Shit. What did he do? Hang up and call the police? Or just bust his ass getting to her house? It would take him at least fifteen minutes to get there, and that was with speeding.

Before he could make a decision, the call went dead.

"Shit!"

Instead of calling her back, he called the police and relayed the little he knew. By the time he got to her place, one police car sat in the front with its lights flashing. He met Officer Johnson inside her apartment. The front door was wide open, and he didn't hesitate to step inside.

"You know, I could've shot you," Officer Johnson said, lowering his weapon when he realized who it was. Mase had met him a few times. His first name was John, which he wasn't a fan of because of his last name. He liked to go by his middle instead, Baxter.

Mase winced, realizing it would've been smart to knock and announce his presence first.

"Sorry, Baxter. Where is she?"

"Still doing a sweep of the place. I had to get Bruce, who manages the property, to open her door. No sign of forced entry—by the front door or the sliding door. All windows here seem to be intact. There is a broken wine bottle in the kitchen."

"She probably hid in her room."

He started for the hallway when Baxter rushed forward and put his arm out to stop him. "I go first, until I know everything is secure. Wait here."

Mase stared at him, a lone brow cocked, telling him that was never going to happen. Until he had eyes on Hope, nothing would hold him back.

Baxter glared in return but didn't say a word. He ventured down the hallway, Mase trailing behind him. It was better he didn't argue with a cop. The bathroom was empty. The first room was also empty, no signs of a broken window. The second bedroom door was closed.

When Baxter tried to open it, he met resistance.

"It's locked."

"She's in there."

He nodded, assuming the same thing he did. She heard a noise, rushed to her room, and locked the door. But why was it so quiet?

"Hope, it's Officer Johnson. You can open the door now."

Nothing.

"Hope. It's Mase. Let us in."

Still nothing.

His heart, already racing a mile a minute, continued to pound frantically at all the possibilities. Was she hurt? Was someone else in there with her? Tyrone? Had he come back and was holding her hostage?

He couldn't stop all the scenarios racing through his mind.

"Hold on." He rushed to her bathroom and came back with a thin hairpin.

It took less than thirty seconds for him to pick the lock. Baxter, once again, put his arm out as if to block him from entering first.

Well, he was the cop. Mase wasn't looking to get arrested tonight for defying a cop's orders.

Baxter twisted the knob and pushed, still hitting resistance.

"There's something in front of the door."

They pushed together, stopping when they heard a muffled sound.

"Hope? Are you okay? Answer me, damn it." He knew he sounded desperate, but he couldn't hide the panic. He needed to see her, to know she was safe and alive.

Out of nowhere, the door opened with ease. Hope stood before them in a funny-looking pair of pajamas, her hair a complete mess, and her stance definitely unsteady.

"Mase? What are you doing here?" She turned her attention to Baxter. "Officer Johnson? What's going on?"

Baxter looked at him for some answers.

Oh, geez. So she was way too drunk, and he called the police for nothing. Just. Great.

"You called me. You told me someone broke in. Then

you stopped talking and the line went dead. I called the police."

Her eyes rounded as if it all came rushing back to her.

"I heard a crash. Like glass-a breaking. Somen did break in. Did you find them?" She shivered, pulling her arms close to her chest, the bells on her shirt jingling.

Mase nearly throttled Baxter as his eyes zeroed in on Hope's chest. Of course, the damn bells had to be over her nipples. Again, he wasn't looking forward to getting arrested, so he kept his comments and his hands to himself.

"The only thing I found was a broken wine bottle. Maybe that's what you heard." Baxter sounded skeptical about everything. He figured Hope broke it, scared herself, and panic-called him, forgetting she broke the bottle herself since she was so inebriated.

"I didn't break it."

"I don't know what to tell you, Hope. There's no sign anyone was in here."

But you were his unspoken words.

She shivered again but didn't say anything. Only the slight jingle from the bells made a sound.

"I'll be going now." Baxter gave him a look as if silently telling him to make sure she didn't cause any more disturbances tonight.

He gave a subtle nod, then turned his full attention to her.

"Are you okay?"

"Yeah, sure, other than I'm the crazy lady making shit up now." A maniacal laugh filled the room as she walked unsteadily toward the bed. "I didn't break no bottle. Wasn't me."

Then she plopped down on her bed. Not even all the way on it. Her feet dangled near the floor.

"We'll talk more about it tomorrow. You need some rest. Can I get you some water?"

She didn't respond.

He walked closer to the bed. "Hope?"

Her eyes were closed and her breathing even. She passed out. Which was probably what happened when she called him.

This was not what he expected to happen at all. A very drunk Hope.

Why?

Because of him? The things they said to each other? Did that mean he meant more to her than she wanted to admit?

Maybe there was still hope for them.

A near heart attack from an intense worry he never wanted to experience again told him enough.

He would fight for her. He'd put his heart through the grinder again if he had to because he would not give up on her.

He positioned her more onto the bed, and then pulled the covers over her, trying not to jostle her too much. The damn bells jingling merrily made him smile, at least.

"Mase..."

He leaned closer, wiping a lock of hair out of her face. "I'm here, Hope."

"Hmm...here. Need you."

There it was again. She needed him.

But in what way? Here he was still trying to define shit.

"I'm not going anywhere."

Although, he did leave the room to lock the front door and clean up the broken bottle. He walked through her apartment, double-checking the windows and the sliding door, finding all of them locked.

So, yeah, she broke the bottle herself. She'd be very

embarrassed tomorrow when it all came rushing back to her.

He found another near-empty wine bottle on the coffee table and put it in the fridge. It proved how much she had to drink tonight. The TV was still on, showing a Christmas movie. He turned that off, then unplugged the Christmas tree, flicked all the lights off, and headed back to her room.

He sent his brother a quick message letting him know where he was but left out the reason why. That would take more than a text to explain.

Then he took off his shirt, shoved down his jeans, and joined her in bed, cuddling her close to his body.

She didn't say anything, but a contented sigh released.

She said she needed him, and he definitely needed her. In the morning, she might not be happy to see him in bed with her. But right now, he didn't care. He needed to hold her close and pretend like everything was good between them.

Maybe tomorrow everything would be much better.

He could only hope.

SHE GROANED. Her head pounded like a herd of elephants were stampeding across her forehead. She didn't even want to open her eyes. The pain wasn't going to be disappearing any time soon.

But she really should take a look because there was an arm lying across her stomach, and she didn't recall going to bed with someone.

Oh, God. Did she call an ex and have pity sex? *Please say I didn't do that. Please, please, please.*

She couldn't do it. She could not open her eyes and see the bad decision lying next to her.

"Can I get you a glass of water and something for the headache you most likely have?"

Oh, shit. It was even worse than she thought.

Mase was in her bed. How in the hell did that happen?

She slowly opened her eyes, squinting at him. One, because she was too embarrassed to fully look at him. Two, because the sun pouring in from the window hurt her eyes.

He looked rumpled from sleep and like he had a long, rough night like her, but he also wore a grin that didn't match his tiredness.

"Morning." He brushed a hand across her cheek before putting it by his side.

She missed the heavy weight of his arm the moment he moved it.

"Morning." She didn't know what else to say. Hell, she didn't even want to know how he got in her bed.

She remembered lots of wine, Christmas movies that made her ache for that kind of merriness in her life, and eating too much junk food.

And her tongue hurt. She vaguely remembered tripping from the corner of the couch and falling.

"Can I get you that water?"

She nodded. Perhaps a moment away from him would give her clarity on what happened the rest of the night.

He rolled out of bed and left the room wearing only boxers.

Did they have sex?

Makeup sex?

Shit, she hoped not because every time with him was magical, and it would suck to think she didn't remember rolling around the sheets with him.

She closed her eyes, trying to think real hard.

Spilled wine bottle. She cleaned it up and came back for her phone, which was when she tripped and bit her tongue. That shit still hurt, even thinking about it. Like the pain happened right in the moment, her tongue started to throb, as if saying 'remember me, bitch, you bit me for no reason.'

A very unsteady walk to her room. Closed the door. A noise.

Yes. She heard a crashing sound. She called Mase in a panic, and then...and then...nothing. She couldn't remember anything after that. But at least she remembered calling Mase, which explained why he was here.

She called. He came.

The man was too good for her erratic, damaged self. He deserved someone better than a drama queen like her.

Covering her face with her hands, she groaned at her stupidity. The fact she didn't remember him coming and what she might've said to him was so embarrassing. She wished she hadn't said she'd take the water. It'd be better if he left to let her wallow in her humiliation alone.

"Here. This should help."

His warm hand on her shoulder was a comfort she wanted to soak up. She didn't deserve that comfort.

"Hope?"

How could she turn his way and look at him? Ashamed didn't even begin to describe how she felt.

"I promise, this will help."

Yeah, it would help her headache, but not how she felt inside. But the sooner she took it, the faster he could leave.

She rolled ungracefully toward him and opened her eyes. His grin was gone, but he still looked tired. The pills disappeared from his hand, and then she drained the entire contents of water. It felt so good to drink an ice-cold drink.

Then she closed her eyes again.

"Thanks for everything."

The bed dipped as he sat down. "Yeah, I'm not leaving if that's what that just meant."

Why did he have to be so damn perceptive all the time?

"We should talk."

"Yeah, and how did the talk you wanted to have yesterday go?" Ugh. Why did she have to be such a bitch?

Just call her a self-sabotager.

"I'll go make you some breakfast. A hot shower might help, too." The bed shifted again as he stood. "Merry Christmas."

She heard his footsteps as he left the room. Shit. It was Christmas Day. In a few hours—who even knew what time it was—she'd have to go to Stu and Chasity's and pretend to be merry and play nice with an asshole who didn't deserve her respect. All of that with a massive hangover.

Shit on a stick.

She missed Christmas mass. How would she ever face Father Benson again?

She stayed in bed, hoping if she laid there long enough everything that happened last night would become a distant memory—and that Mase would give up and leave.

Of course, he could be a stubborn, obstinate man when he wanted to be. He would not be leaving until they had another talk.

She nearly fell out of bed trying to stand up. Her mind was still groggy, not to mention, it still hurt to open her eyes all the way. First grabbing a pair of black leggings and a black-and-white sweater, she then headed for the bathroom. Mase was right. The hot water did soothe her some. By the time she got dressed, brushed her teeth, and combed her wet hair, she felt marginally better. Tomorrow, despite the shops being crazy from after-Christmas excitement, she'd have to buy a blow-dryer. She couldn't live without one.

The smell of bacon drifted her way when she opened the door. It enticed her a lot faster toward the kitchen.

"Coffee's done. Bacon needs another few minutes."

She nodded, grabbed a mug from the cupboard, and poured a cup, sighing happily at the thick, rich taste. He knew how to make good coffee. She didn't dare step any closer to him. There would be too much temptation to ravish him silly if she moved closer. She might not want to have any kind of talk with him, but that didn't diminish how much her body ached to be next to his. If he wanted to chat, they should get it over with.

"Thanks for coming last night. I hope I didn't say anything too crazy."

He turned away from the stove. "Nope."

What? That was it. Nope. He wasn't going to go into what she actually said.

"I spilled wine last night. I should clean that soon."

"I swept up the broken bottle."

She frowned. "I didn't break the bottle."

He mirrored her frown. "There was a broken bottle in the kitchen."

Odd. She remembered throwing the towel in the sink, but she didn't bring the spilled wine bottle with her to the kitchen.

"I spilled it in the living room. I didn't break the bottle in the kitchen."

"There was a bottle in the living room with a bit of wine left. I put it away last night. I guess I don't remember smelling anything. But there was also a broken bottle in the kitchen."

The crash. That must've been what she heard.

"I thought someone broke in. It must've been the bottle."

"You probably dropped it."

The coffee mug slowly lowered as she set it on the counter. It was better she didn't hold a potential weapon as they finished this conversation.

"I didn't break the damn bottle."

Mase flinched.

"You called me in a panic and said someone was in your home. Your words were slurred. I knew you were drunk. You passed out on me and the call dropped. I called the police, I was so worried."

She groaned, burying her face in her hands.

"Officer Johnson had to get Bruce to open the door. I got here as he was searching the house. The only thing we found was the broken wine bottle in the kitchen and you locked in your room. You barely got to the bed before you passed out again."

She got it. She was super-duper drunk last night. But that didn't mean she broke the damn bottle. She knew what she heard, and it was a crashing sound. Somehow that bottle fell all on its own.

She lowered her hands and looked directly at him.

"Are you calling me a liar?"

"No."

But he was calling her so drunk she didn't remember breaking the damn thing. In her eyes, it felt like the same thing. He thought she was lying.

Not only that, the whole town would hear about every little detail by lunchtime. Nothing ever stayed a secret in this damn town. Oh, look, Hope Bronson making a scene once again. Being the screw-up she always was.

"I checked all the windows and doors. They were all locked."

Just more evidence that she was lying. Gee, thanks.

"I don't make it a habit of drinking that much. I had a rough day, okay."

"I'm sorry."

Ugh. Why did he have to be like that? Sound so understanding?

"For what?"

He sighed. "For starting that conversation last night. It was dumb."

"So we're back to being just whatever. No definition."

"No, we're not. I want it all with you. I'm not saying let's move in together, get engaged, and get married. I want to call you my girlfriend. I'm not asking for the damn moon, Hope."

She shivered. Whether from the word girlfriend or the vehement way each word left his mouth. So full of emotion and pain all wrapped together.

"I can't do this right now, Mase. I messed up last night. I'm sorry I called you."

He was in her face in less than three strides, grabbing her hands and squeezing. "Don't ever hesitate to call me. You needed me last night, and I'll always be there for you."

"Even with no definition."

His face contorted into agony. "Even without that. I can't just turn off how much I care about you. If you need me, I'm there."

I need you.

The words sounded so familiar. Had she said them last night?

"Don't be so damn understanding, Mase."

"Are you always this grumpy in the morning?" A grin appeared. "Or is the hangover talking?"

She laughed despite trying to hold it in. "Both."

"Hope—"

"No, me first." Not that she knew what the hell she wanted to say. "I didn't simply mess up last night. I feel like I've been messing up for a long time now. I don't know how to fix anything. I don't know how to shut that bad part of me off." A heavy breath released. "I don't know why I can't give you what you want when I know I don't want to lose you. I can't explain it to you because I can't even explain it to myself."

"You were right last night. I said we'd go at your pace and I rushed you. Let's go back to your pace. All I ever want is honesty from you, and that's one of the first honest things you've told me. I can respect that. I don't want to lose you either. We'll figure this out together."

"I know it's totally last minute, but do you want to come over to Stu and Chasity's house later for Christmas? Your brother and Mia are welcome, too. It's gonna be a real shit-show."

Mase chuckled. "How can I say no to that? We'll be there."

For the first time that morning, her head felt a bit lighter. Like things were starting to look up.

9

HOPE GULPED a large amount before setting the wine glass on the kitchen counter. No matter how much this party made her anxiety crawl, she couldn't get piss-ass drunk like she had last night.

Driving through town, she saw a few odd looks thrown her way. A holiday—where most businesses were closed for the day—did not stop the gossip. Half the town knew she got so drunk last night, she thought the sound of a wine bottle crashing was someone breaking into her house.

How embarrassing.

Although, she didn't care what anyone said—or thought —she did not break that damn bottle. On purpose, anyway. The only thing she could think that might've happened was when she brought the old bottle into the kitchen, she set it too close to the edge and it fell on its own.

But whatever. She wasn't going to dwell on last night. She had to put her armor on and focus on trying not to say anything rude to Mayor Hafferty. He and his wife would be here any minute, and she had to have her game face on by the time they arrived.

Her father was already here. Despite not seeing him often as he had moved out of town eleven years ago when her parents divorced, she still talked to him every so often. They didn't have a terrible relationship, but they also didn't have a very close one either.

It was nice to see him again.

"Why are you hiding in the kitchen?" Chasity bustled into the kitchen with empty hands. She had left a few minutes ago with two plates of goodies to put on the dining room table.

"I'm not. I'm keeping an eye on the ham."

Chasity rolled her eyes. "You're being ridiculous. We have a timer set for the ham. Stu's parents aren't even here yet, so you have no reason to hide."

"I'm not hiding."

Of course, they both knew she was lying through her teeth. In a way, she was hiding. If she could, she'd hide from herself. She couldn't create havoc if she wasn't around herself.

"Do you want to talk about it?"

This time Hope rolled her eyes. Talk about it. What was Chasity specifically talking about? What *it*? The part where she made a mess of things with Mase. The fight they had last night. Her subsequent drinking and the police incident. Yeah, she didn't want to talk about any of it.

"I just want to get through this day."

Chasity walked closer, yet didn't reach out and touch her. "It's Christmas. This should be a happy day."

"I promise to keep my merry smile on my face. Stop worrying about me. I swear, I'm good."

"You're a damn liar and you know it." Yet Chasity let it slide when the doorbell went off. "Enough hiding. Walk with me."

The last thing she wanted to do was argue with her sister. She might not be in the mood for cheery festivities, but she shouldn't put a damper on the day for everyone else. Well, everyone except Mayor Hafferty. She didn't care if she ruined his day.

Following her sister out of the kitchen and toward the foyer, she repeated mentally to *don't be a bitch*. As soon as Chasity opened the door and greeted Stu's parents, Hope knew she'd have to repeat that mantra in her head about every other minute to make it happen.

"Merry Christmas, Hope. Always lovely to see you," Stu's mom, Sarah Hafferty, said with a gentle tilt of her lips.

"You, too, Mrs. Hafferty. What a pretty dress."

And it was. The dress was a deep burgundy that went a little past her knees. Three-quarter length sleeves and a subtle bow near the hip. Stylish and classy. Hope had no issues with Stu's mom. Just his father who was the world's worst selfish, stuck-up boss. Not to mention, he tried to break up Stu and Chasity last year when they rekindled their relationship. Asshole.

"Hope, good to see you," the man she despised said with his fake, cheesy grin that half the town never saw through.

"Hi."

Then she turned around and headed for the living room before anything else came out of her mouth. She was pretty proud of herself for being cordial and greeting him. Sure, it might've left her mouth with a bit of disgust, but she didn't call him any nasty names or ignore him. Win-win in her mind.

They all followed her. When she took a seat next to her dad, she ignored the stern face her sister gave her. Of course, her dad stood up to shake hands and exchange greetings with the Haffertys. As did Stu, who had been chatting with her dad.

Curley, Stu's dog, the stray he sort of hit with his car last year, hopped up on the couch and sat next to her, almost as if he sensed she needed some comfort. She petted him under his chin, giving him the love he deserved and silently telling him thank you.

Hope didn't miss the awkwardness between Stu and his father when they hugged. They had an up-and-down relationship. His father was always trying to push him into a path he didn't want. Like getting rid of the bar. Stu loved that bar. He'd never sell it. All Mayor Hafferty ever saw was how things benefited him. Running for governor, he didn't think his son owning a bar was good enough. From the things Chasity told her on occasion, his father was still bothering him about it. Not as heavily as he used to but enough to continue putting a strain on their relationship.

The doorbell went off again.

"I'll get it." She ruffled Curley's head before hopping off the couch and nearly racing to the door.

At first, when Chasity told her to invite Mase and his family over, it gave her the heebie-jeebies. Inviting someone to your family gathering for the holidays—and Christmas was a pretty big holiday—said a lot. It said that person was important. It said that things were getting serious. It said that she cared way more than she should.

But now she was happy she invited him. He'd be a wonderful buffer and distraction from Mayor Hafferty. Maybe they could even sneak out at some point and do some naughty stuff together. Maybe take a peek downstairs. Stu had an awesome pool table. She'd never had sex on a pool table before. They never did have sex this morning before he left. They should've. That would've been the best

Christmas present she received this year. Great sex with a wonderful man who forgave her for her erratic behavior. What more could she want?

Of course, if Chasity found out she had sex in her house with a bunch of guests in attendance, she'd never hear the end of it. Despite how fun that sounded, she'd be better off staying on her best behavior. Still, having Mase here was a good thing. She'd just ignore what it actually meant for him to come hang out with her family on a holiday.

His handsome smile settled her anxiety as soon as she laid eyes on him.

"We brought some wine and goodies." Mia lifted a nice bottle of red wine that had a delicate white bow wrapped around the top.

"Thanks. What a nice thought." And here came the hard part. "Umm...so yeah, about yesterday."

Jaxson and Mia stared at her, although neither looked upset or unhappy with her. But they did wait to speak.

"I'm sorry for leaving like I did. I should've never done that."

She knew when she was in the wrong, and leaving yesterday without saying good-bye or giving an explanation had been rude of her.

"Don't worry about it." Mia gently smiled. "We all have those kinds of days."

They shared a look. Hope saw the understanding in her eyes, the silent way Mia communicated she had had those kinds of days more than she cared to admit.

"What my fiancée said," Jaxson added, although his smile didn't look as gentle. "Thanks for the invite today."

She nodded but didn't add anything. Mia might've forgiven her, but Mase's brother was an entirely different story. Oh, well, not much she could do about how he felt about her. Other than to try harder and be nice. She was who she was, and unfortunately, she had a hard time changing her bad habits. He had every right to be mad at her for the way she treated Mase. She didn't only walk out on Jaxson and Mia and their company, she walked out on Mase, too.

"You can hang your jackets up here. I'll put this in the kitchen."

She pointed to the closet near the front door, then took the wine bottle and container of what looked to be cookies.

Then she walked away. More like fled the area.

Her mantra 'don't be a bitch' was already failing her. Instead of walking with them into the living room and making introductions, she fled the scene. How could she be so idiotic and rude? What was the matter with her?

Easily remedied.

She set the wine bottle on the counter—sounded more like a slam—and the container of cookies and turned around, colliding with Mase.

"Merry Christmas."

Then he was wrapping his arms around her waist and pulling her closer. His lips touched hers soft and so sweet, she knew deep in her heart she didn't deserve this kind, loving man. She was the exact opposite half the time.

"What was that for?" she whispered, his lips still close to hers.

"I missed you. And I realized I never got a good-morning kiss earlier. I wanted one."

"Oh."

So poetic and romantic. Oh. How much more ridiculous could she get? But he was just so damn sweet all the time.

"We should join everyone. I should be introducing

Jaxson and Mia to everyone. He hates me. Your brother absolutely hates me."

Mase frowned, yet didn't immediately contradict what she said, which meant she was right. Jaxson hated her.

"Stu met us in the hallway. They know Stu. It's fine."

"So he hates me."

"He doesn't. But he doesn't want to see me get hurt."

Hope rested her head on his chest and strengthened her grip. "I would never intentionally hurt you. I swear. I told you I'm a mess."

"And I told you we'd figure this thing out together."

She lifted her head, giving Mase the opportunity to swipe another kiss. Not that she complained whatsoever. Her mind was already drifting to possible places they could sneak away in the house to get it on.

Then she reminded herself that Chasity would disown her if she did something so crazy.

"Come on. We better join everyone or I swear I'm going to drag you off and have my dirty way with you."

Mase chuckled as she led him out of the kitchen, holding his hand. Her grip might've been a touch harder than she needed it to be. But he was her lifeline to staying sane and in control. To keeping her impolite thoughts to herself.

"I wouldn't be opposed to that."

"Don't tempt me."

The sparkle in his eyes said he wanted to tempt her and more.

Oh, this man. He was going to break her sooner or later.

She wasn't sure if that was a good or bad thing.

Mase stayed glued to Hope, not because he felt out of place. Stu and Chasity were very good at making their home welcoming, even with Stu's dad giving off an odd vibe. Not quite mean, but also not inviting. He didn't know how to describe it, and he sensed most of it was geared toward Hope rather than Chasity, which was odd, considering Chasity was engaged to his son, not Hope.

No, Mase stayed by her side because he sensed she needed it. What Hope needed, he was there to provide. While their relationship—or whatever they were calling it —was a bit shaky at times, he wanted it to work. He wanted her.

Forever. Until death do us part.

Not that he planned to say that to her anytime soon. He said he wouldn't rush her, and he planned to keep his word. It didn't mean he didn't envision their future more times than he could count.

He couldn't help himself. He loved her. Crazy, erratic parts included.

While he didn't lie to her about Jaxson not hating her, he wasn't a huge fan of her. Mase understood why. Jaxson was worried about him. At times, he worried himself. Hope had the ability to hurt him like he had never been hurt before.

But he had faith everything would work out.

The evening went well. Conversation flowed smoothly, talking about easygoing topics. Nothing like politics or religion that could stir the pot more often than not. The food was top-notch. The ham was so good, he wouldn't say no if they offered to give him some leftovers. The apple pie was great, along with the other Christmas goodies Chasity had prepared.

All in all, a very nice Christmas get-together. A lot better than he expected, considering the tension he and Hope had this morning.

He believed her that she thought she didn't break the bottle. It broke somehow. If she said she didn't drop the thing herself, then he believed her. The last thing he wanted to do was argue over something silly like that anyway.

When he got home this morning, he gave Jaxson and Mia the short version of what happened. They both chuckled, finding it comical. In a way it was. Not that he'd ever laugh about it to Hope's face. She didn't find anything that happened to her last night funny—more like embarrassing. Since no one had broken into her place, he couldn't do anything but laugh. It was better than worrying that something terrible had happened to her. He didn't even want to think about it.

"This eggnog is so delicious. Better than what we made yesterday. I'm going to need this recipe," Mia said to Chasity, who sat near her on the couch. Stu sat next to Chasity on the other side with Curley on his lap. Jaxson, of course, sat on Mia's other side.

Hope's dad was in the recliner, and Stu's parents were on a small ottoman together. Considering there was no other place to sit, he and Hope sat on the floor in front of the Christmas tree. She was between his legs and leaning back against him. He didn't want to be anywhere else.

"I'll email it to you. It's super easy. I need a refill, actually." Chasity laughed as she stood up.

"Me, too."

He held in his groan as Hope stood up. He didn't want her to leave his arms. It had felt nice relaxing with her. Of course, he knew she'd be right back. There was no need to be clingy.

"Do you want a refill, Mia?" Hope asked.

"Yeah, I'll come with."

"I could use another cup myself," Stu's mother said, throwing her husband an odd smile and then followed the ladies out of the room.

The room was silent for a beat. It felt awkward with only the men left in the room.

He and Jaxson shared a look, but neither decided to start a conversation. He didn't mind Hope's dad. Seemed like a genuine guy. But the only one in the room he felt comfortable with—besides his brother—was Stu.

"So I hear Hope had quite a night last night."

Mase snapped his attention to Mayor Hafferty, his eyes narrowing. He sounded friendly enough, like he was curious about what transpired. Yet the devious look in his eyes was easy to see.

"Yeah, she was concerned someone broke in."

Stu thankfully replied, because, at the moment, Mase wasn't sure what to say. Why was he bringing up what happened anyway? Why did it concern him?

Mayor Hafferty chuckled, half rolling his eyes. "You might want to consider having a chat with her, Stu."

"Why?"

"Calling the police for frivolous things is not a good look."

"She heard a noise that concerned her. Like someone was breaking in. I don't see how that's frivolous," Stu snapped.

Mayor Hafferty stood up. Stu did as well. Mase was teetering on the edge of getting into his face himself. He didn't like where Mayor Hafferty was going with his words. Why in the hell wasn't her father stepping in?

"She was so drunk she doesn't remember breaking that wine bottle. That was the noise. That's frivolous. That's wasting the police's time on something frivolous. It's not a good look."

Mase couldn't take it.

He sprung to his feet and took a few steps toward them.

"I called the police."

Mayor Hafferty trained his gaze on him. "Well, that was quite silly of you."

"She called me first, concerned. Then the call went dead. I was worried about her so I called the police. I'd do it again without hesitating."

"I stand by my words." Mayor Hafferty turned to Stu. "You should have a chat with her."

"Why, Dad? Because it doesn't look good for you, and she's going to be my sister-in-law?"

"I always knew she was trouble. I'm glad I let her go."

Mase scoffed. Hope had told him the entire story when everything went down last year. She had told him why she wasn't looking forward to this Christmas gathering with Mayor Hafferty in attendance. Now he fully understood why. The guy was an asshole.

"She quit last year. It's amazing how you can so easily twist a story to your liking. You're despicable. I'll be sure not to vote for you when you run for governor, and make sure my friends don't either," Mase snapped.

"How dare you." Mayor Hafferty stepped closer. "You're no better than Hope. You're perfect for each other. Two nobodies going nowhere in life."

"And you're an asshole."

Mayor Hafferty poked him in the chest. "Get out of my son's house."

"Go to hell." This man was not going to push him around.

"Knock off it, Dad."

Mayor Hafferty ignored Stu and reached forward once again. Mase wasn't going to stand for it. He shoved the mayor back before he could touch him. Mayor Hafferty stumbled and then fell.

The evil grin that formed told Mase he played right into the mayor's game.

"Call the chief, Stu. I was just assaulted."

"Yeah, call the chief, Stu. My brother was assaulted." Jaxson took a position right next to him. Mase could feel the tension emulating from him.

Stu shook his head, yet didn't say anything.

Mayor Hafferty slowly stood up, holding his hip, like he had hurt himself or something. Honestly, the way he went down, Mase thought he faked the entire thing. He hadn't shoved him that hard, but the man was a devious one.

"I'll call him myself."

"You do that," Jaxson all but snarled. "But don't think for a second you won't be charged with something as well. You touched my brother first. You don't like how Hope makes you look. Imagine what this will look like."

"What's going on?" Mrs. Hafferty asked.

Everyone turned their attention to the threshold of the living room where all the women stood.

"Nothing, my dear. Nothing at all. I think it's time we left."

Mrs. Hafferty frowned, but when no one else said anything, not even Stu who could've so his parents wouldn't leave, she nodded.

They were gone within five minutes with little fanfare.

"So, now, does someone want to tell us what happened?" Chasity asked, staring intently at Stu, demanding he spill everything.

HOPE SAT NEXT to Mase on the couch, silent. She had no idea what to say. The mayor was still the same asshole he always was. This time, actually provoking Mase to get violent with him. That man always had an ulterior motive. He might've left peacefully, but she didn't think this would be the end of it.

"I'm so sorry for my dad. I guess some people don't know how to change."

Hope stared at her dad for a second before looking away. Stu had a point. Some people didn't change. Her father growing up wasn't a terrible parent, but he also wasn't a very involved one. Her mother had always been the one to fight her fights and say what needed to be said. Her dad had always been there, in the background, observing, but never adding his own two cents. Shit never changed. He couldn't even be bothered to stick up for her when someone said things that were nothing but lies.

Yet Mase stuck up for her. He went to battle for her.

She slid her hand into his and squeezed. For the moment, that was her only way of saying thanks. At least, until they were alone together.

"You shouldn't have to apologize for your dad," Chasity finally said. "It's not your fault."

"Yeah, what my sister said." Hope realized she should say something as well. She didn't want Stu to think any of this was his fault either. "I will apologize for my behavior last night, but other than that, nobody did anything wrong but your dad. He can apologize himself. But he won't because he's not sorry."

"Screw that," Mase said with a bit more vehemence than she'd ever heard before. "Don't you dare apologize for anything last night. You thought someone broke in and were frightened. You couldn't have known that wine bottle fell somehow."

He did believe her. She didn't know how much she needed to hear that—to know that—until he spoke with such passion.

"Thank you," she whispered. She had so much more to say, but right now wasn't the time.

"Well," Stu said, standing up from the ottoman, "how about we have another drink and forget this all happened? I learned my lesson. No more Christmas invites to my dad."

"Oh, Stu." Chasity stood up and hugged him.

Hope wanted to give him some reassurance and comfort as well, but she was still reeling from the mayor's nasty words about her and Mase. How dare he put Mase down, too. Mase was nothing like her. He had a successful business and a great head on his shoulders. He was nowhere near the kind of loser she tended to be.

Well, maybe loser wasn't the right word. She didn't think of herself that way. More like, lost and confused. At least for the past year that's how she had felt. So very lost and confused.

"I'll take another drink," Jaxson said with a half-hearted laugh.

Stu nodded, then froze when the doorbell went off. By the frown on his face, he knew it wasn't a good thing.

When Chief Duncan walked into the room with Stu in the lead, Hope knew it was a very terrible thing.

"Mase." Chief Duncan nodded at him, no smile or pleasantries to be found.

Mase stood up as if accepting his fate.

The mayor had run to the chief of police and filed assault charges. The bastard. And on Christmas Day, no less. What a truly heartless man, only looking out for himself.

Jaxson jumped to his feet. "You put handcuffs on him, Chief Duncan, and you better be ready to put some on the mayor of this town as well. He put his hands on my brother first. My brother was only defending himself. I want to officially press charges against him."

Hope stood up as well. In fact, everyone in the room was standing, even her father. He might've not said anything before—and technically still wasn't—but at least he stood in solidarity with them right now.

"No official charges have been filed, although I did receive a visit from the mayor. He's asked that you leave town. Not return."

Jaxson put his hand out for Mase to not say anything.

"Again, I'd like to file charges against the mayor for assaulting my brother. Because if that man thinks he's going to threaten my family and get away with it, he's wrong."

"I was a witness. He put his hands on Mase first," Stu added.

Chief Duncan nodded, then the start of a smile appeared. "Oh, I knew he wasn't an innocent man in the entire thing. I wasn't telling Mase to leave. I was telling you what the mayor asked me to tell you. Screw him. He's messing with my Christmas festivities, and I don't appreciate that."

Hope felt Mase visibly relax next to her.

"So, what are you going to do, chief?" she asked, hoping it was something to tear that man down a peg or two.

"Well, I can file a report." Chief Duncan shared a look with Jaxson. "He'll most likely file one in return."

"That's fine. He can do what he needs to do," Jaxson

replied, not sounding a bit worried about his brother and his possible fate in the situation.

"Yeah, it's about time my father has a mark against his name for something. He started the fight. He said things he shouldn't have said. Anything that happens from this moment on is his own fault. He's the one who had to go to you and think he could threaten someone without any consequences. It's ridiculous how much he thinks he can get away with."

Hope let out a silent breath, shocked, yet humbled by Stu's words. She knew it wasn't easy for him to say any of that. He might have a tumultuous relationship with his father, but the man was still his father.

"Okay. Tell me everything that happened, and I'll file charges."

Hope didn't want to hear it all again, so she quietly left the room while Mase, Jaxson, and Stu relayed everything that happened.

Chasity and Mia joined her in the kitchen a few minutes later.

"You okay?" Chasity asked, coming to stand by her.

She shrugged. "I'm fine. It's Mase who has to worry."

"He shouldn't worry. Jaxson won't let anything terrible happen. And if it goes very far, like actual court, Jaxson will make sure he has the best lawyer there is," Mia replied. "But, based on the little I know of the mayor, he won't want any of this to go to court. I'm sure it'll all die down soon."

Chasity nodded as if agreeing. "This is a way to show the mayor that he can't keep shoving everyone around and keep getting away with it. He'll get served a summons. I highly doubt Chief Duncan will arrest him. He'll file counter charges against Mase. Before things escalate, I'm sure they'll both come to an agreement to drop the charges. But it'll be too late for the mayor because it'll be a red mark on his record. Not a good look for a man running for governor. Perhaps he'll finally learn to stop pushing people around."

"This is all my fault. Mase getting into trouble once again because of me." Hope looked at Mia. "You know he was arrested a few months ago because my ex-boyfriend got into his face. He got into a fistfight with him over me."

"Mase is a big boy and makes his own decisions. You're not making him stick up for you. It's obvious why he keeps doing it." Mia tilted her head and smiled.

Chasity even wore a secretive smile.

Hope frowned and took a step back as if these two were preparing to fight her.

"Like what?"

"Oh, my gosh. My sister is not that dense. That man loves you, so accept it and stop acting like a drama queen with the man." Chasity rolled her eyes for good measure.

"I do not act like a drama queen." Oh, she so did. That was the biggest lie she had told so far.

Mia giggled.

"I don't," Hope insisted. Then she huffed because she could. "Okay, fine. I get a bit dramatic sometimes. But he can't love me."

"He can and he does," Mia said seriously. "If there's one thing I know about the Brandt men is once they fall in love, they fall fast and hard. They don't give up. They don't give you space. They refuse to let you win the internal battle you're most likely having with yourself. I should know. I battled hard with myself before finally caving and loving Jaxson with all my heart. I did not make anything easy on him."

"I'm a screw-up. I'm lost. I don't even understand my own feelings." She could feel tears battling behind her eyes, but she would not lose that battle. She would not cry on Christmas.

Chasity stepped closer and wrapped an arm around her. "You're not a screw-up. You're brave and courageous. You don't let people walk all over you. You're a strong, badass woman. Own it. I'm proud to call you my sister. I'd be lost without you."

Well, damn. She couldn't hold her tears in when her sister said such wonderful things. A few escaped, trailing down her cheeks. She wiped them away before hugging her sister fiercely.

"I don't know what I'd do without you either. I wish I could make all these feelings disappear."

Chasity squeezed her tighter. "Those feelings make you who you are today. Don't wish them away. Embrace them."

How did her sister get to be so wise?

They let each other go. Hope didn't miss the way Chasity swiped at her cheeks as did she one more time as well.

"So, this is the most intense Christmas I've had in a long time. I should tell you the story about the time I went to a work party with my bestie Gabby. Oh, boy. It was insane."

Chasity grabbed the pitcher of eggnog and refilled their glasses. "I love a good story. Say the word and I'll pull out the shot glasses. We can really have a party."

The ladies clinked glasses and laughed.

Perhaps this holiday wouldn't be a complete shit-show.

Not with good friends and her family by her side.

10

JAXSON GLANCED UP THE STAIRCASE, then back at him. Mase knew he wanted to say something without Mia around while he had the chance. He might as well get it over with.

"Get it off your chest."

Jaxson sighed. Oh, not a good sign for Mase. But that didn't hold Jaxson back.

"You sure you're going to be okay?"

Mase cocked a brow. "Yeah, why wouldn't I be? The charges the mayor filed against me have been dropped. The charges we filed against him were dropped. Everything is back to normal."

Kind of.

The last two days since the Christmas incident had been a whirlwind. Jaxson and Mia were supposed to leave yesterday—the day after Christmas. But when the mayor filed counter-charges, Jaxson extended his trip, not wanting to leave until things were semi-settled. Thankfully, they were all the way settled.

The mayor was served a summons. He was served a summons. This morning, Chief Duncan had dropped by saying the mayor was willing to drop his charges if Mase was willing to drop his as well. They both signed an agreement that neither would take action—criminal or civil—against the other. The mayor wanted to brush it all under the rug like it never happened. Obviously, the man didn't think Mase would do something about it. He thought Mase would just leave town with his tail between his legs. Nope. Not how he operated.

Of course, he didn't want to take things any further. He had only wanted to show the mayor he wouldn't be pushed around. He signed the agreement after Jaxson and Mia looked over the document as thoroughly as he did. There didn't seem to be any weird loopholes he had to worry about.

It was all over.

Except the part concerning him and Hope. Since the moment they left Stu and Chasity's house on Christmas, he had only spoken to Hope via text. A few random messages here and there. Nothing too extreme. Definitely nothing about where their undefined relationship was headed.

Jaxson sighed again when Mase didn't elaborate anything further. Oh, Mase knew what Jaxson was really talking about.

Hope.

It always came down to Hope.

"You're sure you know what you're doing?"

"Are we going back to that?" Mase crossed his arms. "Where you try to talk me out of seeing Hope."

"You have gotten in trouble with the law twice now because of her."

"Neither was her fault."

He'd argue that point until he was blue in the face. The first time he got into a fistfight with her ex was because her ex wouldn't leave her alone. Not to mention the guy took a swing at him first. He wasn't going to stand there while some dude beat the shit out of him. Hello, it was called self-defense.

Again, this time around, the mayor started it as well. If the man hadn't gotten into his space a second time—most likely to poke a finger at him—he would've never pushed him away. Nobody was going to touch him without consequences.

"I'm not trying to talk you out of seeing her."

"Sure in the hell sounds like it."

Jaxson stepped closer and lowered his voice. Not that they were raising their voices, but he figured Jaxson didn't want to take the chance Mia would hear him. She probably told him to stay out of it.

"I'm worried about you. I don't want to see you get hurt. That's all. I swear I'm not trying to persuade you into leaving her."

Mase stared at him for a moment, processing his words. He had a point. He didn't want to see himself get hurt either. When it came to Hope and the way she felt, the way she didn't want to define what was between them, in all reality, he *would* end up getting hurt.

It sucked.

No, it royally sucked.

Yet, he had to take the chance. Wasn't that what love was about? Taking a chance. Taking a leap of faith. Believing that love would win in the end.

He'd like to think so.

His parents had a good marriage. Sure, he knew they had their ups and downs, as all marriages did. No relationship was easy. It took hard work, patience, and communication. He was willing to put in the work. Hope was worth it.

The question was, was she willing to put in the work as well?

"I don't want to leave with you pissed at me."

Mase finally cracked a grin and slapped his brother on the shoulder. "I'm not pissed. I get what you're trying to say. But I love her. I can't just walk away from her. If she ends up doing the walking, then that's what brothers are for. To have my back. To cheer me up."

Jaxson nodded. "I'm always here for you."

"I know you are. I'm always there for you. I'm glad you stayed the extra day, despite the reason for it. Summer can't come soon enough."

"Oh, you're excited about shopping for suits for my wedding." Jaxson laughed. "Our friend Dominic is a whiz when it comes to clothes. It'll be an easy thing."

"I miss New York. It'll be nice to be home. It's nice to have an excuse to come home. Sometimes it's hard to get away."

Although his brother was getting married in September, he wanted to be involved in as much of the wedding plans as he could. Considering he was the best man, that meant he had to be there for quite a few things. Living how many states away made it hard, but he'd do what he'd have to do to make it work.

"Yeah, you work too much."

Mase rolled his eyes. "Like you don't?"

Jaxson only chuckled, because he knew it was true. Crime didn't sleep, and as a homicide detective with the NYPD, Jaxson was always busy, always being called out for one crime or another. Mase didn't know how Mia did it. That had to be hard on a relationship.

Their attention was diverted by sounds on the steps.

Jaxson rushed forward and grabbed the suitcase Mia was lugging down the stairs halfway.

"I would've brought it down."

"Don't be silly. I was up here." Mia looked at Mase. "I think I packed everything, but if I missed something, bring it with in June, if you don't mind."

"Of course. If it's something super important, I'll mail it."

Hugs went around as they said their good-byes. Mase helped Jaxson put the bags in his truck and grabbed more hugs before they finally backed out of his driveway. The drive to the airport went quicker than he wanted. He'd miss his brother. More hugs went around when he dropped them off at the departure area. He waved good-bye as they walked into the airport and disappeared out of his view. The drive home felt like it took a lot longer than the way there.

When he got home and shut the door, the silence gave him goose bumps. For the past week, beautiful sounds filled these walls. Laughter and lively conversation.

He was thankful his brother had been able to stay as long as he had. Mase knew it couldn't have been easy getting that much time off around the holidays.

Now silence.

He pulled out his phone to check the time.

2:33 p.m.

Too early to call Hope as she was still at work until five.

Not that they had to be together every single day, but he wanted to see her tonight. He wanted—

Well, he shouldn't bring up the whole relationship conversation again, no matter how much he wanted to.

He told her he'd let this thing between them go at her pace and he had to stick with it. He would not rush her.

Perhaps he'd surprise her at work when she got off. He'd

pick her up and bring her here for a romantic dinner or something.

She said she was confused about her feelings. He had to help her unravel them and make them make sense.

He had to woo her.

Like, full non-stop wooing.

Christmas was over, but that didn't mean he wouldn't use some of the holiday spirit still lingering in the air to help him.

His tree was still standing tall and proud in his living room. The lights were still strung on the house outside, looking pretty.

He had tons of leftover Christmas treats from Jaxson and his mad baking skills.

He could do this.

Operation Holiday Hope commenced.

Because he'd still use the Christmas cheer to help woo her and pray on a little bit of hope it would work out in his favor.

───

"HEY, YOU'RE OFF EARLY," Theresa said as she bustled behind the counter and grabbed the coffee pot, assuming Hope wanted a cup.

She wouldn't say no to one, although it wasn't the reason she stopped by.

"Thanks." Her hand curled around the hot mug as Theresa put the pot back on the coffee burner.

"What's up?"

Thank goodness for good friends knowing there was a problem.

"So many things I don't know where to start."

"Is this about the wine bottle incident, the mayor incident, or did something happen with you and Mase?"

Hope chuckled, hating how Theresa hit them all on the head.

"Well, people are still commenting to me about how much I enjoy my liquor a little too much. 'You don't want to become an alcoholic, Hopey. It's not a good look.' I wanted to puke on Marybeth's shoes when she said that to me yesterday." Her hands tightened around her mug. "And she knows that I hate it when she calls me Hopey, and yet she still does."

"Because she's a pest and loves stirring the pot. What a bitch."

"Next time I'll say that to her. I walked away instead."

"Probably for the best. Marybeth looks for that attention. By not giving it to her, you aggravated her."

Hope chuckled. "Good." Then she took her first sip of the coffee and winced.

"Yeah, I know. Terrible pot today, more so than other days. My back is killing me, and I'm tired today."

"Can I help?"

Theresa waved her hand in the air. "No, I'm good. You're off early for a reason. Spill."

Hope shrugged. "Not really. Father Benson said I could go early because I'm caught up with everything. I have everything scheduled for the New Year's mass. I've even started getting things ready for Lent."

"Girl, you are on top of your game. Talk about organized."

"I like things to run smoothly. What can I say?"

"Well, on to the next thing then."

Hope rolled her eyes. "The mayor incident. Yeah, not many people have said anything about that. I think they're still trying to process the fact he's not as perfect as they thought. I ran into Councilwoman Waters, and she said I'd make a wonderful mayor. That I should 'boot that self-absorbed ass out of office.' How ridiculous is that?"

Theresa didn't say anything at first, looking contemplative.

See, Hope knew it was the silliest thing she had ever heard. Even her friends didn't think she was capable of something that huge.

"You'd make a wonderful mayor. You love this town. You love the people. You're friendly and outgoing and you don't stand for bullies. Not to mention, having worked for the mayor, you know how the office runs. You'd be perfect for it."

"Do you really mean that?"

"I would never lie about something like that. I'd vote for you. Plus, he's trying to run for governor next year. We need a new mayor. Good riddance, I say."

"Well, I definitely won't be voting for him for governor."

"Same."

They laughed together, then silence surrounded them. Theresa was probably waiting for her to address the third issue, and Hope wanted to ignore that one altogether.

Mase.

And what they really were?

"So, we've concluded Marybeth is a bitch and you're not an alcoholic, or on the verge of one." Theresa smiled wickedly, trying to gain a smile out of her, which worked. "You're running for mayor. I will definitely help with the campaign."

Hope laughed but didn't say anything. She wasn't sure she'd do something so out of her wheelhouse.

"That only leaves one thing."

Hope looked down at her coffee, then took another sip, despite the rancid taste. It was soothing in a way. A familiar taste. A comfort because one could always rely on Theresa to never change.

Sometimes, she worried she never would either.

Which meant her relationship with Mase was doomed to fail. They always did with her.

"Something happen between you two?"

Hope shook her head. "He left that night with us on good terms. It's...he wants to define us, and I want..." She shrugged and looked at Theresa. "I want it to work out, but I'm scared. It never works out for me."

"You've also never dated a good, nice man before. That's the difference."

Theresa made such a good point.

It was still scary as hell. Probably even scarier than running for mayor.

"Seriously, you'd help on my campaign."

Theresa leaned forward with the gleam in her eyes. "Every single step of the way. And hey, I bet Emma would totally be on board, too. The things she's done with Lynn's bakery, setting up the website, selling goodies galore all around the world. She has some mad business skills, or design skills or whatever you want to call it. She'd be perfect for your campaign manager. Have you seen the new website for Betty's Craft Corner? Amazing. It's so pretty and makes me want to buy all the beads on there. It's so tempting."

Hope hadn't seen the new website Emma had designed for Betty yet, but she knew Theresa wasn't exaggerating. Ever since Emma jumped all in on designing websites and also local advertisements around town, she'd been busy. Everyone wanted her help for this and that. She had a keen eye and good ideas simmering away in that head of hers.

"I'll keep it in mind."

"I won't say anything to Emma." Theresa smiled deviously. "Not yet anyway."

"Give me time to think about it," Hope said with a nervous laugh. "It's a lot to think about."

"You have more to think about than just that. Don't think I didn't notice how you switched the conversation from Mase."

Yeah, because she didn't want to think about him.

"My time here is up. I should go."

Theresa gave her a stern look mingled in with a smile. "Sure, you can leave, but don't think I won't bug you about it again. He's a good guy. Give him a decent chance. You're hurting both of you."

"Stop being so wise, Theresa. I can't stand it."

Hope paid for her coffee, thanked Theresa for putting it in a to-go cup, and headed out into the blistering cold. No snow in the forecast, which was a great thing, but it was brutally cold out.

She made it home shortly after, chugging down the nasty coffee in quick order. She grabbed some water from the fridge before grabbing a notepad.

Pros and Cons of becoming mayor

She stared at the header until her eyes started to blur. Her hand didn't move. Nothing went under the title.

~~**Pros and Cons of becoming mayor**~~

That was too involved for her to even think about right now. Her mind was racing with other things where she couldn't focus on that task.

She had to focus on the only thing that would help her determine that list later.

She started giggling as she wrote out MASH under her previous scribble. Then she started labeling other items on the paper: where I live, what kind of car, how many kids, what kind of job, who I marry. Her hand trembled as she wrote the last one. Then she filled in every category with four things.

Her choices to live were Mulberry, of course, Hawaii, Europe, and Timbuktu. If she was going to play this silly game, she would have fun doing it. She tapped her chin as she thought about cars. It didn't matter to her. She listed four kinds of cars, one being a truck, and her own, of course, and moved on to how many kids she'd have. She listed zero, two, five, and ten. She seriously hoped she didn't get ten.

For jobs, she listed her current job, actress—it was always a dream of hers—waitress, and finally, mayor.

Her hand trembled once again when she got to the married part. Then she quickly scribbled three celebrities that she had huge crushes on—because a girl could dream if she wanted to—and jotted down Mase's name last.

Now for the number. She hadn't played this silly game since middle school with her friends. Normally, one of her friends provided the number and then she'd start counting and scratching off the items as the number landed on them.

She shot her sister a quick text.

Give me a number between 1 and 10.

Chasity: Why???

Because I need one.

Chasity: 😒 You're so weird sometimes.

Number please!!!

Geez, why did her sister have to prolong her misery?

Chasity: Fine! 9

Thanks. Love you, bye!

She tossed her phone to the other end of the couch and decided ignoring her sister's next text would be the best thing. She was too embarrassed to admit she was playing a childish game to see if she and Mase were compatible.

Because, honestly, how much more childish could she get? She was being utterly ridiculous.

But it didn't matter. She started the game and now she had to finish it.

She started counting to nine, crossing off things as she hit the pinnacle number.

She could only hope her life on this piece of paper turned out awesome.

11
_____

MASE BLEW OUT A BREATH, then knocked on the door. He knew Hope was home. Her car was clue enough, plus the lights blazing outside through the windows. At least, he hoped she was home. It would make it that much harder to track her down if she wasn't.

He figured out, after a very embarrassing chat with Father Benson, that she left work early. Who knew a priest could have fun teasing someone and making them sweat? Mase couldn't believe how many questions Father Benson asked him before he finally confessed Hope left early.

How was your Christmas? Did you go to mass? Have you said your prayers today? Have you seen the beautiful pictures the children drew last night hanging on the wall in the hallway?

So many different questions he had a hard time keeping up with Father Benson.

His Christmas was...different, yet enjoyable. He did not go to mass. His cheeks had burned hot when he told the truth he wasn't too good about attending mass regularly. That put Father Benson on a separate tangent on how important going to mass was. Yeah, he said a few prayers. Not that he told Father Benson what kind. Father Benson would not want to know his biggest prayer was that Hope gave him a chance. And no, he had not seen the pictures on the walls. He'd be sure to do so on his way out.

Finally, after a bazillion questions and answers, Father Benson asked how he could help him. Mase simply had wanted to see Hope.

"Oh, she left early today. She's not here."

All of that and he didn't even get what he wanted. Of course, he'd never be rude to a priest, so he chatted amicably for a few more minutes and then excused himself.

It wouldn't have killed him to pull his phone out and text or call her, but she had a tendency to....well, lie to him when she felt threatened. It was best to show up and ask her to join him for supper in person. He wasn't sure why he was nervous she'd shut him down, but it swirled in his veins he was on the verge of losing her.

If he ever really had her to begin with.

The door finally swung open, and he didn't miss the flash of surprise in her eyes.

"Hey."

He could work with that greeting.

"Hi. Are you busy? Am I interrupting anything?"

Her eyes got large for a moment before she shook her head. "Just chilling. Come on in."

He grinned as he followed her inside where she beelined it to the living room and grabbed the things sitting on the couch.

"I hope I'm not interrupting you."

Because he had the feeling, the way she clutched the notepad and pencil in her hands, that he had.

"Nope. Not doing anything important at all. Very lazy night."

He nodded, yet didn't believe her. Hope was the worst liar on the planet.

"So, you don't have plans?"

"Do you have something in mind?"

"I was thinking supper. At my place. If you want to."

Why did things feel awkward between them? Everything was good when he left on Christmas, despite everything that happened. He kissed her good night, said he'd see her soon, and he left with her smiling and waving good-bye.

Yet a weird, awkward tension filled the air.

"Supper sounds good. I haven't eaten yet. Let me change."

Before he could tell her she was fine in her leggings and T-shirt, she skirted out of the room like someone lit her on fire.

So odd.

But she didn't say no, and he could officially start Operation Holiday Hope and woo the woman he loved permanently into his arms.

She came out a few minutes later wearing jeans that made her ass look so damn tempting to grab and a blue sweater that fit every curve with delight. Damn, she made him horny as hell with one simple look.

"What?" She swiped a strand of hair behind her ear as she laughed nervously. "Did I get makeup on my sweater or something?"

Her eyes trailed down, her hand swiping at her shoulders as if she saw dirt or something.

He stepped closer and brushed a hand across her cheek, prompting her to look at him.

"You are the most beautiful woman. You look amazing."

A gentle smile appeared, her eyes lighting with pleasure. "You always say the sweetest things."

Then he was doing something right.

"Come on. I have food in the oven and I don't want it to burn."

"So you knew I didn't have anything going on tonight."

"I *hoped* you didn't have anything going on tonight."

Her smile brightened as she put on her coat and grabbed her purse. "You could've called me earlier."

Yeah, and risk her declining his invitation as she'd done in the past? No, thank you.

"I wanted to surprise you."

He exited first and waited while she turned out the lights and locked up.

"I'll drive and bring you home later." *If you want* were the words he kept to himself. If everything went accordingly, she'd be spending the night.

Every single night.

Okay, he might be pushing where things were going tonight, but a guy could hope.

The drive to his place was smooth as was the conversation. The weird tension in her apartment had dissipated. Perhaps he had imagined it.

When he pulled into his driveway, he didn't miss her wide smile as she gazed upon the lights lit on his house.

"I'm going to miss the Christmas lights. I think that's my favorite part about the holidays. All the pretty lights that people put up."

Who knew? Wait until she stepped inside his house.

He forced himself to remain calm and aloof and not grin like a damn teddy bear. As soon as he unlocked his door and stepped to the side for her to enter first, he heard her audible intake of breath.

"What is this?" She looked back at him as he closed and locked the door.

He shrugged. "A little extra merriness." He blew out a breath, wondering if he should even say anything.

With the question in her eyes and the way her smile disappeared, he knew he had to.

"Christmas Eve and Christmas Day were...not what I envisioned."

Her eyes drew to the floor. "I'm so sorry about Christmas Eve. I should've never left."

"It happened and it's over. Besides the mayor acting like a jackass, I enjoyed Christmas Day. This is my way of adding a bit more cheer that I feel like we missed."

She looked at his living room once again where he had added white lights around the room. They had been a bitch to hang, but worth it by the way her eyes lit up with pleasure as she walked farther into the room and twirled around to look at it all.

All the lights were off besides the ones hanging on the walls and the Christmas tree lit up. It gave it a nice, romantic feeling. Exactly what he wanted.

He had a vase of red roses on the coffee table, a small string of white lights wrapping haphazardly around it.

"The flowers are for you."

She set her purse down, took off her jacket and shoes, and then picked up the roses and inhaled.

"I can't remember the last time I got flowers." Her eyes closed and she inhaled again. "They're so beautiful. Thank you, Mase."

She set them back down and sniffed once more.

"What smells so amazing?"

"Lasagna?"

He said it questioningly because he had no clue whether

she liked it or not. It was an easy meal to make. The only annoying process to it was how long it took to cook.

"I like it."

Although, now that he thought about it, he should've done spaghetti or something. They could've done the whole noodle thing where they each ate an end until their lips met. That would've been romantic. Or weird. Why would they eat the same noodle? They would've had separate bowls.

Whatever. She liked lasagna and he wouldn't worry about it.

She was here now, and he should go with the flow and stop overanalyzing every little detail.

"Do you want a glass of wine?" he asked as he took his jacket and shoes off and put them away.

"I'd love one."

She followed him to the kitchen. He couldn't help the smile that broke free when he heard her gasp again.

"More flowers. You're spoiling me."

He watched as Hope walked around the kitchen smelling the two other vases filled with roses. He'd spoil her for the rest of his life if she only gave him the chance.

The wine bottle was already uncorked—he liked to be prepared—and he poured them both a glass.

"Why don't you have a seat and I'll get the food. It should be done."

He let her go through to the dining room first and chuckled when she snapped her head back in his direction.

"How am I going to get all these flowers home?"

Every single vase he bought today had been worth it. The joy and happiness in her eyes was something he'd always remember. Two more vases of roses sat in the middle of the table along with two candles he planned to light.

More white lights were also strung around the walls, giving off that romantic glow.

As long as the evening continued to go in his favor, she'd find two more vases of roses upstairs in his room. For good measure, he had three more in his workshop, in case they made a trip out there for some reason.

"I hope you like roses. There were so many options, but in the end, I loved how they looked."

They were all fresh and beautiful smelling, he honestly couldn't pass them up. Although, he had felt slightly bad, considering he bought the entire stock in the store. He didn't think the florist had minded though.

Hope set her glass down and walked closer. "They are my favorite flower ever. At least, they are now."

Then she kissed him. A strong, heavy kiss that told him he had done everything exactly right.

His cock jumped to attention, pressing into her. Her low moan that escaped said she wanted more like he did.

"Do you want to see what's upstairs?"

She giggled against his lips. "What, did you put flowers in every single room?"

"Maybe."

She brushed her hands through his hair, kissing him deeply one more time. "Feed me first. Then give me a tour."

"Your wish is my command."

The sad part was, she didn't realize it.

He'd do anything for her.

THIS MAN COULDN'T GET any sweeter.

As Hope took a sip of her wine—she wasn't indulging tonight—she decided, nope, he could get so much sweeter.

"Why are you looking at me like that?" Mase asked, reaching out his hand to grab ahold of hers. His fingers started to brush her palm, sending pulsating tingles straight to her core.

Damn, he knew how to work her up with little effort. Shit, she had wanted to jump his bones the moment she saw the first vase of flowers.

"Just admiring how sweet you are."

"Oh, keep going."

She giggled along with his boisterous laugh.

The night had been wonderful. Definitely not what she had on her agenda, but she was so glad he decided to surprise her. After ruining Christmas Eve, the dumb mayor acting his usual jackass self, this low-key special night helped make her Christmas feel a little brighter.

Mase could cook. The lasagna had been pure perfection, as well as the garlic bread he had thrown in the oven for a few minutes before they sat down to eat.

The wine was delicious, and the company couldn't be beat.

"Thank you for this."

"Thank you for coming." Then he grinned crookedly. "I do have another Christmas present for you."

Her cheeks bloomed and grew hot. She had brought presents for all four of them on Christmas Eve. Mase had been thoughtful enough to bring them with him to her sister's house where he, Jaxson, and Mia had opened them. Cam had taken his home on Christmas Eve. It hadn't been much, especially with such short notice. She had gotten Mia a spa kit. Bubble bath, nail polish, and a candle that said it gave off a soothing aroma or something like that. She had secretly bought herself one, too. It sounded relaxing.

Jaxson got a fun mug with hot chocolate mixture in it. So

lame, but she didn't know the guy. At least, she got him something. It was the thought that counted, right? Cam got the same thing. Next year, she'd do better for both of them.

And Mase had been the hardest to buy for. What do you buy for a man where you don't want to define the relationship? Not something small, but also not something too expensive. Finding something in the middle had been near impossible.

Until she saw a neat leather tool belt in Bernie's Hardware Store. Mase's had looked worn down and she thought a new one would do him well. She might've even hid some interesting sex toys in some of the pockets. She knew he noticed them at her sister's because his cheeks had flamed red, but he didn't pull them out. Perhaps he would a little later.

He had given her a beautiful shelf that she had already hung up in her bedroom. It was the perfect spot to put a frame of her and her mother on. He didn't need to give her anything else. Because she knew the time and hard work he had to have put in making the shelf. It was already enough.

This supper was enough.

"I don't need anything else."

"I know, but I already bought it and..." His eyes held a bit of worry. "And I want you to have it. It doesn't have to symbolize anything. Just know that."

Oh, dear. That didn't sound good.

He let go of her hand, and she immediately missed his touch. Part of her felt like she needed him to hold her hand for emotional support. So damn silly. Why did she always have to be so irrational about things, even in her own head?

He left the room and came back less than a minute later. Not enough time for her to mentally prepare for what he was about to give her. He set it in front of her.

Well, it wasn't a ring. That was good. But it was jewelry.

She opened it, inhaling a deep breath.

A silver necklace with a teardrop diamond sat on a velvet mat. It was simple, yet exquisite. She didn't deserve something so lovely.

This didn't symbolize anything? Ha! He was so delusional. This said too much. It had girlfriend, super-serious relationship stamped all over it. Hello, big neon flashing lights pointing at what it said.

"Hope? I need you to say something. Anything."

His nervous chuckle had her tearing her gaze away from the necklace.

"It's beautiful. It's too much."

"Wear it. Don't. It's yours. I saw it and I felt compelled to get it. I knew it would look perfect on you."

Mase was a good man. How many more examples did she need?

She picked it up, holding it delicately in her hand. "Thank you."

Then she put it on.

His eyes glittered with delight. "God, you're gorgeous."

And she was an idiot.

For resisting him for as long as she had. For making things difficult every step of the way. And for what reason? Because she didn't understand her own emotions.

Well, she was starting to get a better handle on them.

Mase was opening her eyes a little more by his sweet actions tonight.

Her silly game might've helped, too.

"I have one more present for you, too." She laughed, putting her hands over her face. "You're going to laugh at me, but I want to show you."

"Show me?"

She held up a finger for him to wait and dashed out of the room. Her hand shook as she dug for the notepad she was doodling on earlier. Her legs might've even wobbled—definitely felt like jelly—as she walked back into the dining room.

His brows rose as she put the notepad in front of him and took her seat.

"What is this?" He chuckled, picking it up.

He flashed the pad at her. "Why is my name on here with celebrities? I should be happy my name is circled and not crossed off like theirs, right?"

"Oh, yeah, definitely happy."

She threw her hands over her face again, embarrassed she was even sharing this with him.

"Hope."

The ache in his voice, plus the understanding had her lowering her hands. He took one of her hands into his.

"It's called MASH. A silly game kids play to see what their future will hold. I don't know what came over me to play it today."

Mase looked at the paper. "MASH. I've never heard of it."

"Girls probably play it the most. You put a bunch of different things you'd like in life and then pick a number and count, crossing off anything the number lands on. Look," she said, pointing at the A. "I live in an apartment. Which is too bad because I would've loved to get the mansion." Then she glided her hand to the 'where I live' part. "Somehow I end up in Europe. Yay. I've always wanted to travel there, not sure how I feel about living there." Next, her finger went to 'Car I have.' "Of course, out of all the choices I wrote down, I get stuck with my beater of a car. I mean, it's not terrible, but there's no fun in that." Her finger hit the kids and job part. "Apparently, I'm going to have five kids. Still debating if I'm terrified or excited about that. And my job leaves me confused because, oddly enough, I had hoped it would land on something else."

He squeezed her hand as his smile increased. "My name is circled, too. So I'm a part of this future you have."

She bit her bottom lip. "You are. I'm sorry a silly game had to help make me see that. And confirm it."

"And if it would've landed on Ryan? I'd be shit out of luck right now."

She giggled, her heart slowing down a bit that he was laughing with her and not reacting in a completely opposite way. "He is my favorite actor. I would've suffered living without you, but also jumped at that future."

His laughter filled the room, then he lifted her hand and kissed the back of it. "What part of this is my present?"

"I guess the part where I say let's define us. Like, you can call me your girlfriend and I won't get all weird about it."

He pulled her hand until she stood up, and then she was on his lap and in his arms. A light kiss touched her lips.

"Best damn present I got this year. I promise I won't rush you into anything. Let's see where we go with this."

"Well, apparently, we'll be living in an apartment in Europe with my old-ass car, five kids, and I'll be working at a church."

Mase's lips brushed hers once again, so tenderly and soft, she ached for more. "Sounds like the perfect life. Because I have you."

Damn. This man and his sweet, sweet words.

"So you would've been happy with the shack, too?"

He chuckled. "Is that what the S stands for? Yeah, even the shack. I can build things pretty well. I'd build us the best damn shack there was. I guess H means house."

She nodded.

"Well, lucky me I got picked over Ryan and those other two celebrities."

No, lucky her. Except she couldn't say so because his lips were back upon hers.

She needed more. She needed to tell him she meant business. Perhaps her body could do the talking for her.

"Mase, give me that tour now."

He smiled against her lips before kissing her thoroughly one more time. "You got it."

Then he stood up with her still in his arms. She had a secure hold around his neck, although she didn't worry he'd drop her as he climbed the stairs. This man had muscles galore. She didn't consider herself fat, but she also didn't think she was light enough to be carried upstairs.

She almost blurted out 'I love you' when she saw more roses in his room. Baby steps. She committed to labeling their relationship; she wasn't ready to admit she loved him yet.

"Gosh, you shouldn't have spoiled me so much."

"You deserve it."

Then they were removing each other's clothes and falling gloriously naked in bed together. Mase did the wonderful things he knew how to do with his tongue. Touching her in places she had no idea would feel so blissful. When her first orgasm hit, the smile on his face said he planned to beat his old record of how many times she could come.

"I love the sounds you make when you hit your peak. You're so damn beautiful." He moved slowly up her body, kissing her softly. "Say you'll spend the night."

Her heart skipped a beat, a moment of panic hitting her. Not that she had never spent the night at a guy's house before, because she had. Yet it felt different with the quiet, almost insecure way he asked.

Her hands wove through his hair and down his back. "I'd like to see you try and kick me out."

She said she wanted to label this relationship, and girl-friends stayed overnight at their boyfriend's house. It wasn't a big deal. She would stop making these moments a big deal.

His lips curled up in delight before he kissed her, telling her just how much her words meant to him.

The heat in the room inched up in slow increments as he peppered kisses all over her body once again. His mouth made a trail down to where she knew she'd come again from the delicious way his tongue could move, but she wanted more.

She pulled on his hair. "Condom, now. I need you."

He looked up at her, his eyes shimmering with an emotion she couldn't quite decipher. Then he was grabbing for a condom and rolling it on, the moment over for her to ask what the look had meant. Knowing her, she wouldn't have had the courage to ask anyway. She didn't want anything to ruin this beautiful moment.

He entered her slowly, holding still for a few seconds when he was all the way inside, kissing her.

"I shouldn't say this, but you mean everything to me. I need you, too."

Before she could even say anything in return, his lips were on hers, as if trying to silence her, and he was thrusting in and out.

She held on for the sudden wild ride he decided to take them on. In and out so passionately, she knew this was going to be the best sex they'd ever had to date.

His kisses lit her body on fire as did the intensity of each thrust. So deep and hard, she never wanted the moment to end.

"Oh, Mase, I'm so close," she whispered breathlessly between the erotic kiss they couldn't seem to stop.

"Yes," he all but growled before moving his lips to her neck, then lightly biting her ear.

She grabbed his ass, digging her nails in as he kept pumping hard in and out.

"Damn, I'm close, too. Too close." He lifted up, finding her sensitive spot as he pounded into her a few more times, then tensing.

His face contorted into beautiful bliss, yet he kept rotating his fingers until she finally came along on the ride with him.

He collapsed into her arms, his lips coating her neck with soft kisses, his breathing hard and heavy.

"So, so beautiful," he whispered into her ear.

"And you're so perfect. Thank you for such a wonderful night."

"My pleasure." Another kiss hit her neck. "Always my pleasure when it comes to you."

Oh, yes, she'd gladly take any pleasure from him any time, any place.

She should've put a label on them right away. The sex went from great to beyond amazing.

What a great Christmas it turned out to be after all.

12

THE DOOR SHUT with a slight heaviness to it. Mase looked up from the project he was working on. Cam looked okay, yet the way he closed the door said something was bugging him.

"Hey, man." While they were best friends, sometimes Cam could be closed-mouth about things. It bugged him, yet he got it. Just because they were best friends didn't mean he had to be privy to everything in Cam's life. He wouldn't pry if Cam didn't want to talk about whatever was bugging him.

"What are you working on?" Cam asked, his brows furrowed as he looked at the large piece of wood lying on his bench.

"Well, remember when I was telling you two days ago that Hope was thinking about running for mayor in Mulberry?"

Mase was still shocked by her confession. She had confessed the night they made their relationship official. Of course, he supported her in any direction she decided to take her life. She wanted to be mayor? He'd cheer, campaign, and help her in any way he could. Making signs seemed like the best place to start.

Cam nodded, glancing at the wood again. "You're making her a sign. This thing is huge."

Mase grinned. "Whenever she finds herself a headquarters for her campaign, she needs a nice-looking sign for it. She doesn't know I'm working on it."

He loved seeing her expressions, especially when he surprised her with things. Like the necklace he had given her. Her eyes had been filled with awe, happiness, and a touch of trepidation, as if she were scared of going too far in their relationship. He'd let her have her moments of panic, but he wouldn't let her get away.

She was the one. He just had to prove it to her.

"She's going to love it. You do wonderful work."

Mase chuckled, setting down the tool he was using, and headed for the fridge. "You want a beer?"

Mase didn't bother telling Cam he did amazing work as well. Cam knew, yet in that simple sentence, Mase had heard a hint of vulnerability. Something was going on with his friend, and he wasn't sure whether to press or not.

"Yeah, a beer sounds good."

He popped the caps off the bottles and handed one to Cam. "You okay?"

Cam shrugged before taking a long swallow. "It's been a long day. That kitchen I'm remodeling right now is a pain in my ass. She wants this color of cabinets, then switching out from a Shaker-style cabinet to a glass one. I nearly blew up at her today, but somehow managed to keep my cool when she changed her mind for the billionth time. I mean, come on, it's New Year's Eve, and I did not have to come running when she called. She better not call me tomorrow. I won't answer."

Mason nodded with a slight chuckle. He understood what Cam was expressing because he had those kinds of clients before, too. And if they didn't want a red mark against their company—those bad reviews that hurt—they had to suck most of the shit up and complain to each other.

His bad mood made sense now. That would put him in a sour mood, too.

Cam shuffled his feet, picking at the beer label. "I might've made an ass of myself, too."

"With the cabinet lady from hell?"

Did they have damage control to do? Sometimes they swapped projects if one of them couldn't stand the client any longer. Mase would take one for the team if Cam needed a breather from the woman.

Cam looked up. "I saw Serenity at the floral shop in Mason when I was walking out of the hardware store earlier."

Mase arched his brows when Cam stopped speaking. He waved his hand in a circle. "And? Dude, what happened?"

"I stopped to say hello. Introduced myself, telling her I was at the snowman contest in Mulberry. Congratulated her on her win." Cam shook his head, running a hand down his face. "She looked at me like I was a stalker."

Laughter floated out before he could stop himself. It wasn't funny. His friend decided to take a chance and ask out a woman—he assumed Cam had wanted to build up to that—and he fumbled instead.

"Dude, it wasn't funny. I explained it all wrong when I was talking about the contest. She looked at me weird, thanked me, and walked away like she couldn't get away fast enough from me." He took another long swallow. "I completely screwed up."

"Maybe you'll see her again and it won't be as awkward next time. Hope knows her. We could always—"

"Yeah, no, I'm good. Don't tell Hope, please. It was embarrassing. Please, dude. Don't say anything to Hope. My pride is wounded right now, but I'll get over it."

Mase nodded, not wanting to push. "I won't say anything to her."

There were some things a person didn't have to tell their significant other, one of those things was confidences between best buds. Cam had had it rough in the romance department. He fell in love with his high school sweetheart, they went to the same college, they had plans to get married ——until she decided to give him a big ol' screw you. She cheated on him with his best friend from high school. Not only did he lose the love of his life, but he lost his best friend, too.

Mase had been there to help him pick up the pieces. They graduated college together, decided to open their own business, and the rest was history. Now Mase was his best friend, and he'd do anything for Cam. Even not telling Hope things that shouldn't be a big deal. But Cam asked him not to say anything and he wouldn't.

He was proud of Cam, though. Since the break-up ten years ago—which was the same amount of time they'd been in business together—he hadn't dated much. Sure, he took a few women out here and there, but nothing serious ever developed. The fact he tried to approach a woman who had two kids said Cam liked her a lot. He wouldn't ask out a woman with that kind of baggage unless he liked her.

"So you coming to the party tonight?" Mase asked, hoping Cam wasn't going to let this rejection hurt him from having fun.

It was New Year's Eve. He had to come. Aiden and

Theresa were throwing a party. Their first time having people over for New Year's Eve—so he was told by Hope. He didn't know who all was going to be there, but he imagined Chief Duncan and his wife Lynn, and Chasity and Stu, for sure. It didn't sound like they were throwing a huge party, but also not super small either.

Cam shrugged. "I don't know. Maybe."

He glared at his friend, shaking his head. "Come on, man. You have to come. It'll be fun."

"I'll feel like a third wheel."

Again, Mase didn't know everyone coming, but it couldn't be all couples.

"You won't be. It's New Year's Eve, you have to be there. Ring in the new year with friends."

He stared hard until Cam started laughing. "Okay, fine, twist my arm. I'll be there. You're driving me home because I plan to drink and have fun since you insist."

"Call me DD. I'm your man."

Boisterous laughter filled his workshop. It was good to see his friend laughing again, not the sullen cloud that had been hanging over his head when he walked in. He didn't mind being the designated driver if it meant his friend had a good time. Anything to get him out of his sour mood.

Tonight would be a good night.

HOPE TOOK a sip of her coffee, only wincing slightly at the flavor. Actually, not a bad pot from Theresa today. Emma took a sip of her tea before picking up her pen, poised for action.

"Let's do this."

Nerves started to take over, coffee nearly spilling over

the rim as she set the mug down. "Maybe we should do this later. And not at the diner."

Emma looked around, cocking a brow. "Umm...this place is empty because the lunch rush is over. Stop making excuses. You called me two days ago about being your campaign manager, and I'm all in. This is exciting. I've never done anything like this before, but I swear, you won't regret it."

Hope wasn't sure whether that was true or not yet. She might regret it. What made her think she had the capability to be mayor of this town? She had no experience in politics. Well, besides being Mayor Rafferty's secretary for four years. Her specialty was floating around from job to job, doing the best she could at whatever position it might be.

"You're going to be great at this," Emma assured her, as if sensing she needed that reassurance. Unfortunately, Hope did. She needed a boatload of reassurances.

She was in way over her head.

"This is a mistake. I have a good job at the church." The MASH game even confirmed that's what she was meant to do in life. How could she ignore that?

Emma rolled her eyes, as if reading her mind. "You are not basing your future on a silly childhood game. Because if we did do silly things like that, I'd be back with my ex-boyfriend, Jared, with three kids living in a shack. No, thanks. I'll stick with Bentley, my beautiful toddler Tuck, and the wonderful house we live in."

Hope snickered, almost snorting she laughed so hard. "You totally played it after I told you what I did."

"I couldn't help myself. I burned that shit so Bentley didn't see it." Emma leaned forward. "It's a game. It doesn't mean anything. We make our own destinies. You're meant to be mayor. I can feel it in my bones. You're a wonderful person, Hope. Always helping others, always there for your friends. You know the ins and outs of city hall because you worked there. You got this. Me, on the other, would never do it because I'm so not a people person. You are, though."

Emma leaned back, taking another sip of her tea, giving her time to let everything sink in with what she said.

She made all good points. But it was scary to venture out and try something new. What happened if nobody voted for her? Well, besides her friends and family. She knew she had their vote. What happened if she did win and she completely failed at the position? She wasn't that old, only thirty-four. She didn't have an enormous amount of life skills behind her back. People might think she was too young for the position. Too stubborn on certain things and too unfocused on others. She could be the completely wrong person for this job.

"I already took the liberty to find out who else is running next year. There's only one other name on the ballot. You have to run."

Hope's hands curled around the mug. "Who? I didn't think anyone else had stepped up yet since Mayor Hafferty is running for governor next year."

"I'm coming. I'm coming. Wait for me."

Emma and Hope watched—holding in their giggles—as Theresa waddled with a pep in her step toward them.

"I have everything cleaned up from the lunch rush, and now I can join the chat. What are we talking about?"

Hope scooted over so Theresa could sit. She sat sideways, her belly sticking out instead of being crushed by the booth table. Hope couldn't hold in another giggle at the adorable way Theresa sat.

"I know. I look ridiculous."

"You look cute. Stop it," Emma said with a stern tone.

"We were talking about Hope's campaign and why she needs to run for mayor. She has to boot Mayor Hafferty out of his spot."

Hope leaned forward, nearly knocking her coffee mug over as her hands hit the table. "Shut up. He is not running. He's running for governor."

Emma shook her head as a wily smirk emerged. "Oh, no, he's not. He backed out yesterday. I couldn't get much out of anyone at city hall, but I figured it's due to the little red mark against his record, getting a summons for assault."

"Dirty bastard thinks he can run again and continue controlling this town after what he did. Everyone's starting to see his true colors. He's a snake hiding in a good suit." Theresa pursed her lips in a frown as she rubbed her belly.

It was such an odd combination. Looking so angered, yet motherly.

"I can't believe it." Hope sank back into her spot. "He's running with his tail between his legs. He honestly thought he could say or do anything he wanted and make his way without an issue. I'm glad he's not running for governor. It would've killed me knowing he was in such a high position."

"What are you going to do about it now? Keep hedging whether you'd be good at the job, or knock his ass out of the seat? They don't have limited terms here, and he's been mayor for far too long. It's time someone else held the reigns," Emma said with confidence as if she knew without a doubt Hope could win.

"It'll be a battle. He's not going to make it easy on me."

But what did she care? She never backed down from a fight. She could be downright pigheaded, refusing to bow to people's feet.

"You know you have tons of people behind your back

supporting you. You can win," Theresa said with as much conviction as Emma had.

"Where do we even start?" Hope asked, deciding she was doing it. She couldn't back out now. Not knowing Mayor Hafferty was sticking around. She couldn't wait to wipe off the smug look on his face.

"I'd like to help."

All three women turned their attention to Marybeth, who stood near the door. They were about three booths away, but as no one else besides Bonzo was in the diner, they hadn't bothered talking quietly. Funny how none of them heard the tiny bell above the door ding when Marybeth opened it.

She walked closer to them, smiling her normal smooth, confident smile that always grated on Hope's nerves.

"Help with what?" Hope decided to play dumb. Marybeth was the last person she wanted help from. More than likely she'd try to sabotage her campaign from the inside because that's the kind of devious person she was.

"With your campaign for mayor."

"Who said—"

"I'm not dumb, despite what people think about me." Marybeth pressed her lips together, as if forcing herself to hold her tongue and not get into what people thought about her. "I've heard rumors around town you've been thinking about running. You just confirmed it when I walked in. I heard you."

Shit. Hope wasn't sure how she felt about the town knowing she was planning on running for mayor. How did they even find out? Maybe Emma let it slip yesterday when she visited city hall. By the shock in Emma's eyes, Hope didn't think so. She wouldn't reveal her secret so soon.

Maybe Emma showing up asking questions got the rumor bug started.

Who was she kidding? Not much stayed a secret in this small town. It was bound to get out sooner or later, especially since she had to start campaigning now if she intended to beat Mayor Hafferty next November.

"Why would you want to help me?" She and Marybeth had never gotten along. They weren't in the same grade, or even in school at the same time as Hope was older than Marybeth by five years. But Marybeth had a way about her, rubbing everyone the wrong way.

Marybeth glanced between all three of them before landing on Hope once again. She swore she saw a hint of vulnerability in Marybeth's eyes before it vanished as if never existing.

"My daddy is on the city council. I do know a thing or two about how the place operates. I'd like to help."

That didn't answer Hope's question about *why* she wanted to help. What was her endgame?

"Sure, when we get everything up and running, I'll call you," Emma said before Hope could decline Marybeth's help. She wasn't sure having Marybeth on the campaign was the best thing.

"Perfect." Marybeth's triumphant smile grated on Hope's nerves for some reason. "Have a wonderful day, ladies."

Then she left, swaying in the only way Marybeth knew how to walk. As if every single man—married or not—was watching her walk.

"Why did you say that?" Hope asked harshly.

"Please," Emma said, cocking a brow and waving a frivolous hand in the air. "You always keep your enemies close, keeping an eye on them. You say no, and who knows what the hell she might do."

Theresa nodded. "Good point. Give her a simple task, like putting signs in people's yards or something."

They all busted out laughing, imagining such a picture. Marybeth would balk at such a menial task.

"Oh my God, I'm doing this, aren't I?"

Both ladies nodded with wide, brimming smiles.

Then Emma picked up her tea and held it out. "To a happy New Year."

Hope clinked glasses with her as Theresa mocked clinking an imaginary glass.

Yes, it would be a happy new year. She had so much to look forward to.

A new job.

A new relationship.

Basically, a new beginning.

She couldn't wait for the challenge everything would bring.

13

THE KNOCK on his workshop made him jump. He placed a hand over his heart, laughing, as Hope walked in.

"Shit. Am I late?"

He glanced at the large clock on the opposite wall, noting he was definitely not late. There was still another hour left for him to work before he had to stop, take a shower, and pick up Hope.

She was early. And not even adhering to their plans. Why did she drive to his house? Was something wrong? Did she change her mind about them and was breaking it easy here instead of in front of their friends?

When she didn't answer his simple question—it had an obvious answer by looking at the clock—his heart started to pound a little faster than it already was.

He set down his tool and took a few steps toward her. "Is something wrong?"

She shook her head, glancing from him to the sign halfway finished, then back to him. "Is that for me?"

Another silly question, considering he had engraved 'Hope Bronson for Mayor' on it.

"It was supposed to be a surprise."

She stepped closer, grazing her hand over the top. Then her hand smoothed a path from his cheek, landing on his chest, the same place he had touched himself when she startled him.

He knew she could feel the rapid beat of his heart by the way her eyes rounded, the questions filling her gaze.

"Sometimes I can't believe how lucky I am. You know you're too good for me, right?"

He placed his hand over hers. "Are you kidding me? You're about to be mayor of a town. You're going to be too good for me."

Leaning in, he kissed her. His hand still held hers, while his other one made permanent residence on her hip.

"You didn't answer my question. Is something wrong?"

She sighed. "No, it's been a long day. Emma is like a drill sergeant. I think I've created a monster. The list she has already made for the campaign is insane."

"You'll win by a landslide with her behind the wheel."

"I hope so." Nervous laughter escaped. "Mayor Hafferty pulled out of the governor's race. He's going to run for mayor again."

Hmm. So something was wrong. She was worried.

"You'll knock him out of the park. I'll be right by your side the entire time."

"You're like my own personal hero. My knight in shining armor. Sometimes I wonder if you're even real."

He chuckled, snatching another kiss because he could. Because he loved feeling her lips upon his.

"I'll always be here for you. I'll do anything for you. Are you worried about running against him? Because I wouldn't be. He's not going to win. Not this time. You have a lot of people in your corner, not just me."

Her eyes shimmered with unshed tears. "I know. I can't believe it sometimes."

"You need to believe in yourself more often."

"I feel like life has beaten me down so many times, it's hard to. That's why I panic about things. That's why I make erratic decisions sometimes. I'm sorry for all the pain I caused you getting my shit together."

"But it's together, so that's all that matters."

"I don't want to hurt you."

Oh, she was scaring him again. What did that mean?

Her hand escaped from underneath his. She wrapped her hands around his neck and yanked him toward her. Her lips scorched his, the kiss almost bruising. He felt her pain, her rage, her deep, deep anguish in the fiery kiss.

She let go as fast as she had latched on.

"What was that?" he asked breathlessly, ready for round two, despite almost losing his breath from the intense kiss.

"I'm scared shitless. About everything. About us. About running for mayor. About how Father Benson is going to take it when I tell him I have to quit. Yet, I'm excited, too. It's a new year tomorrow, and I want to start off on the right foot."

"Okay. It's good to start the new year that way."

He didn't know what else to say. His heart was still beating a mile a minute, afraid she was teetering on the edge of calling things off already. He barely had her to begin with. A few days of claiming her as his girlfriend.

"I'm saying I'm ready for a new start."

"That's good." As long as she wasn't breaking up with him.

She slapped another strong kiss to his lips, laughing. "You're so adorable all confused and worried. I'm totally making a muck of this. I was getting ready for tonight, excited for the new year, and I had to see you. I couldn't wait. I didn't even finish curling my hair."

Mase took a quick look at her hair, which looked perfectly fine to him. She wore a knit hat, and the few waves he could see were pretty, lying gracefully over her large winter coat.

"You're beautiful."

"And you are the most patient man in the world to deal with me. I love you and how you take care of me." She flashed a hand at the sign on the table. "Look at you already making this beautiful sign. I could've changed my mind, and you're already jumping in without testing the temp of the water."

His hands tightened on her waist. "Back up a moment. What did you just say?"

She bit her lip, a smile hiding behind the gesture. "You're always putting me first and doing your best to treat me right. It's my turn to put myself out there first. I love you. And I know you said you're prepared to stand by my side as mayor, but I have to make sure."

This time, he crushed her lips with his own, letting all his emotions break free with the kiss. It turned so hot, he picked her up and set her on the bench, stepping between her legs, showing her how much he loved hearing those words.

"I love you, too. It's been really hard holding that in. I said I wouldn't rush you and I meant it."

"Well, I'm not saying let's move in together yet, but..." She shrugged, an almost shy, tentative smile gracing her lips, so unlike her. "I wanted you to know how much I care about you."

"This is the best damn New Year's Eve ever."

"Better than Christmas, for sure."

He chuckled, kissing her again. "So, we still have some time before the party."

Her eyes glimmered with desire. "We sure do."

Clothes fell away quickly as he showed her truly how much hearing those three simple words meant to him.

"YOU LOOK HAPPY," Chasity said, stopping next to her with a fruity drink in her hand.

Hope was impressed by the party so far. Theresa and Aiden went all out. Stu even offered to run 'the bar' for them. They had a nice tall table set up in the corner of the room where their Christmas tree usually sat, acting as a makeshift bar. They had all kinds to choose from. Hard liquor, wine, beer—you name it, they had it. The dining room table was filled with food that Hope was full simply looking at it all. Music played in the background, and everyone was chatting away, happy and carefree.

They invited the usual gang they hung out with. Bentley and Emma, Elliot and Lynn, and Theresa's brother James and his wife, Erin, were in town for the holidays, so they were here, too. Cam had ridden with them, chatting with some of the guys from the firehouse where Bentley worked. A few cops—not on duty—were also in attendance. Serenity and a few other ladies around town were also here. Thank goodness she didn't see Marybeth, at least.

All in all, it was a great turnout.

Chasity bumped her shoulder when she didn't respond. "Spill?"

"What?" She had no idea what her sister wanted her to confess.

"You look happy."

"So you said." Hope rolled her eyes. "It's been a good day."

"Is that all?"

She took a sip of her fruity drink—a Bahama Mama— before responding. "I'm ready for the new year. There's a lot on my plate."

"You have my and Stu's vote. You're going to kill it. I know it hurts Stu the way his father acts, but he doesn't deserve to be mayor anymore."

"I appreciate the support. I know it can't be easy on Stu."

"I don't think their relationship is ever going to get better, until his father acknowledges his part in everything. Which the man seems incapable of doing."

"I saw him in town today. It was *awkward*," she said, emphasizing the last word. Awkward didn't even begin to describe it.

"What did he say to you?"

"That I'm living in la-la land thinking I'll win." Hope smirked behind her glass before taking another sip. "I could see him shaking in his boots. I can't wait to take that asshole down."

Chasity clinked glasses with her. "I can't wait to see it. Don't tell Stu I said that."

She made a sign as if zipping her lips. Hope figured Stu thought the same thing, but the man was his father; he would never vocalize it.

"So things are good between you and Mase? Everyone likes him."

Her gaze glided to him chatting with Cam and Aiden over by the bar, while Stu did his thing making signature drinks like he was born to do it. She figured he was since he owned a bar.

"I love him."

"Whoa!" Her sister took a step back, her brows rising in disbelief. Then Chasity tried to feel her forehead. "Are you sick? Are you feeling well?"

She rolled her eyes, scoffing. "You're so hilarious. I can properly express my feelings sometimes."

"And when are you going to tell him? This is great. He's a good guy. He'll treat you right. Not like all those other assholes you dated."

"I told him earlier. He said it back."

They squealed in delight like they used to growing up sharing stories about boys.

"It's going to be an amazing new year for you. I'm so proud of you, Hope."

That was so great to hear from Chasity, especially since she couldn't hear it from their mom. Having lost her six years ago from a heart attack had been difficult. Thank goodness she had Chasity and her grandpa to get her through it.

They shared a hug, wiping a few tears away before anyone else saw.

The night went by fast. Mingling and laughing and playing silly games as the clock ticked closer to midnight.

There were only two minutes to go when she and Mase took their spot behind the couch, a glass of champagne in their hands, waiting to ring in the new year.

She saw Mase glance over to where Cam and Serenity stood, smiling, leaning into each other.

"Oh, is love in the air?"

Mase shrugged. "Maybe. I don't know. This is the first time I've seen them talk tonight."

She pinched his butt, chuckling when he jumped. "What aren't you telling me?"

His cheeks bloomed a rosy red. "Nothing to tell. It'd be nice to see Cam with a good woman."

Hope nodded. "She is super nice. Also super busy raising twin boys. Is he prepared to date a woman with kids?"

She didn't know Cam well, but considering she was looking at a happily ever after with Mase, she would eventually get to know him.

"He's cautious with women, having been burned before. He knows what he's doing. They're only talking."

Aiden suddenly turned the TV volume up. "It's almost time. Let's start the countdown."

Mase turned toward her, wrapping an arm around her waist. "To a beautiful new year with the most amazing woman. I love you."

"I love you, too. I can't wait to see what this year brings."

Ten...nine...eight...seven...six...five...four...three...two... one!

Then Mase's lips were on hers and everything else faded away.

Cheers to a new year! One filled with love, happiness, and new challenges to overcome.

DON'T MISS THE NEXT BOOK IN THIS HEARTWARMING HOLIDAY SERIES!
SLEIGH ALL THE WAY

OH, AND DO YOU WANT TO KNOW MORE ABOUT JAXSON & MIA? THEN CHECK OUT - THE RIGHT TIME

For Elliot & Lynn's Story
Merry Me
A Holiday Romance Novel, #1

He never knew a simple gift left on his porch step would mend his wounded heart.

Hiding his dislike for the holidays isn't easy, especially when Chief Elliot Duncan meets a woman who captures his attention with one sweet smile. Lynn Carpenter is beautiful, strong-willed, and hardworking, and he doesn't know how to return her gift that was left on his porch by mistake. As Christmas approaches, it doesn't take much for the holiday spirit to seep in, not when Lynn makes it so effortless with her excitement. The only thing he wants for Christmas this year is her heart. But between his meddling father and the need to take care of her, something she passionately resists, he knows it won't be that simple. He's up for the challenge, because losing Lynn is unacceptable.

FOR AIDEN & THERESA'S STORY
MISTLETOE MAGIC
A HOLIDAY ROMANCE NOVEL, #2

A mistletoe. A kiss. This just might be the start of a beautiful Christmas.

Theresa might not make the best pot of coffee in town, but people still flock to the diner for a cup, even Officer Crowl, who rarely displays a smile since his fiancé died. She'll never be able to win his heart, but it's hard to resist him, especially when he kisses her under the mistletoe. Well, on the cheek, but that has to count for something...right?

Staying busy keeps Officer Aiden Crowl sane. Because when he's idle or alone, he thinks, and nothing good comes from that. Everyone thinks he's the perfect man. They think he's broken because she's gone. He is, just not for the reason they believe. Every time he walks into the diner, one sweet smile from Theresa erases some of the pain. He should stay away from her. Far away. But what is he supposed to do when they're standing under a mistletoe? Kiss her, of course.

What if you had one wish granted for Christmas? What would it be?

Acting reckless isn't something Bentley Wilson is known for, but when he runs back into a burning building to save a little girl's puppy after specifically told not to do so, that's exactly how most of the town sees him, especially the fire chief who insists he has to help with the annual Christmas party because of his behavior. Throw in the fact the woman he's pined over for too long is getting married, this holiday is going to go down as one of the worst. Until he meets Emma Brookes. She's feisty, headstrong, and holds so much pain hidden in the depths of her beautiful green eyes. He wants nothing more than to erase her sadness. But it's already a season of disaster, and every time they're together, they spar like two warriors dueling to the death. Despite that, he likes the challenge, the crazy way she makes him feel. Before the holiday is over, he vows to get his one Christmas wish. That she never leaves his side.

FOR JAMES & ERIN'S STORY
SNOWED IN LOVE
A HOLIDAY ROMANCE NOVEL, #4

A blizzard. A cabin. A cup of hot chocolate.
The perfect mixture to fall in love.

James Brennen is nothing but a screwup. At least, in the small town of Mulberry, that's what everyone thinks of him. As a recovering alcoholic, he's trying his best to turn his life around, to be a better man. All of his hard work comes crashing down when he's fired from his job at the hospital— accused of stealing drugs. Nothing ever changes and he's done trying to prove himself. Needing time alone, his friend's cabin in the middle of the woods provides the perfect escape. He knows he's found deep trouble, not only when he gets stranded during a brutal snowstorm, but that he's stuck with the one woman he's wanted since the first day he laid eyes on her. The passion burns bright between them, but it doesn't matter, because as soon as Christmas is over, he's leaving for good.

FOR STU & CHASITY'S STORY
SNOWFLAKES AND SHOTS
A HOLIDAY ROMANCE NOVEL, #5

One last shot at love...

Stu doesn't have many regrets in life—not even the fact he
never decorates his bar for the holidays. But when a bar
fight turns into needing medical attention, he's put face-to-
face with the one woman he's tried to avoid for the last
fifteen years. Okay, so maybe he regrets a few things. He
should've never walked away from her. It only took a good
knock to his head to make him see clearly. He's going to win
Chasity's heart once again. It doesn't matter that she's not
going to make it easy; he's up for the challenge. Bring on the
bets and all the Christmas spirit he can handle. Except, one
person doesn't like the idea of them together—the same
person that had him walking away from her all those
years ago.

For Cam & Serenity's Story
SLEIGH ALL THE WAY
A HOLIDAY ROMANCE NOVEL, #7

There's no such thing as too much holiday cheer...right?

If there's one thing Cam is good at, it's working with his hands. So making a sleigh for the woman who loves Christmas with a passion seems like a foolproof plan to win her heart. He's done being stuck in the friend zone. Except he's a little rusty with dating. After keeping women at a distance for so long, he's going to need more help than he realized. Who knew he'd get it from where he least expected it—her twin boys. This should be easy-peasy. But one thing Cam has learned: nothing ever works out like he plans.

Serenity doesn't like it known, but she hates Christmas. With a passion. The last thing she can do is let anyone know, especially her boys. She'd never ruin the holiday for them. Besides faking holiday cheer, she finds herself having to resist the one man who is impossible to resist. Cam is everything she always wanted in a guy: kind, caring, always there for her when she needs him. But they're friends, and losing him from her life can't happen. Venturing into the sex-zone would ruin it all. If there is one thing she's good at, it's pretending. All she has to do is make him believe being friends is for the best.

DO YOU WANT TO KNOW MORE ABOUT JAXSON & MIA?
THEN CHECK OUT...

THE RIGHT TIME
A PERFECT FOR YOU NOVEL, #2

The plan: Organize an epic birthday party without spilling the massive secret—that has nothing to do with the party.
Time Frame: Two weeks.

Plan a party? Check.
Try not to think about the man she can't have? Check.
Suddenly accept said man's proposal. Check.

Wait...what did Mia Carter do? There was no way she could marry Jaxson Brandt. It would never last. Nothing in her life ever does. They weren't even dating. They couldn't go from just friends to marriage. She'll just have to tell him she changed her mind. If only he'd give her a chance to do so. But between planning a birthday party and trying to keep her bestie from finding out they're getting hitched, she can't seem to find the right time. He's making it his mission to show her what love is truly about—something she'd never had before. She's just not sure it'll be enough to convince her.

ABOUT THE AUTHOR

I'm a *USA Today* Bestselling Author that loves to write contemporary romance and romantic suspense novels, although I am partial to romantic suspense. I even dabble in paranormal. Honestly, I love anything that has to do with romance. As long as there's a happy ending, I'm a happy camper. And insta-love...yes, please! I love baseball (Go Twins!) and creating awesome crafts. I graduated with a Bachelor's Degree in Criminal Justice, working in that field for several years before I became a stay-at-home mom. I have a few more amazing stories in the works. If you would like to learn more about me and my books, head to my website by scanning the QR code. Thanks for reading!

Scan me